The Headmaster's Daughter

CRAZY
HORSE

Crazy Horse Press
116, Bewdley Road, Stourport,
Worcs DY13 8XH
Tel: 01299 824858
email: phayden@crazyhpress.demon.co.uk
website: www.crazyhpress.demon.co.uk

© Peter Hayden 1999
ISBN 1 871870 09 7

Cover pic: Natalie Roguszczak, © Lucy McDermott

Gen. information –
first year = yr 7 (11-12), second year = yr 8 (12-13),
third year = yr 9 (13-14), fourth year = yr 10 (14-15),
fifth year = yr 11 (15-16).

Printed by T. Snape & Co Ltd., Boltons Court, Preston PR1 3TY. Tel: 01772 254553 Fax: 01772 204697

Foreword

The main characters in this book are:

Pupils:
    The 'ordinary' pupil . . . . *Kay Downes*
    Her older sister
    (ex-head girl) . . . . *Liz Downes*
    The gambler . . . . *Paul*
    The head boy . . . . *Brendan Price*
    The headmaster's daughter . . . *Adrienne Appleby*
    The rebel . . . . *Vlad*
    The library helper/fusspot . . . . *Janey*
    The girl with the walkman . . . *Lindy*

Teachers:
    The head who dies . . . . *Mrs Threadgold (Goldie)*
    [Her daughter, a singer . . . . . . *Kate Nantucket*]
    The acting (stand-in) head . . . . *Mr Dooley*
    The new head . . . . *Gordon Appleby*
    The English teacher . . . . *Mr Bowering*

Other characters:
    Kay's mum, a teacher . . . . *Mrs Downes*
    Brendan's mum,
    a school governor . . . . *Gloria Price*
    Candidate for the head's job . . *John Olney (Fido Dido)*
    Chairman of D.I.Y. store . . . . . *David Humbolt*

The book was conceived and written in collaboration with a fourth-year (yr 10) class. I took them to hear Berlie Doherty talk about her book, 'Tough Luck', which she wrote with a class from Doncaster. On the way back, someone suggested that as I wrote books, I should try the same thing.

Writing by vote is quite tricky. For example, when the group voted on the kind of book they wanted, the most popular choices of subject were sex/dating, horror/murder, and ordinary school life. When they voted on style, humour came out way in front. So I had to write a funny book about ordinary school life, sex and dating, with murder and horror included ...

In the end we got it down to a plot where a head-teacher dies (I didn't have time to spend weeks researching police procedures, so they let me get away with death by natural causes); the new head is not popular, but has a beautiful daughter who comes into the school as a fourth-year. All the lads want to pull her, but are wary of her dad.

When the group voted on characters, two of the most interesting were the 'better' – a boy who is always involved in card-games and gambling – and an average/ordinary pupil who doesn't often get noticed. I made them quite important in the book: in fact the average pupil is the narrator, the person telling the story.

The people who were most involved in the development of the book were:

Fay Bethel
James Colclough
Helen Chance
Vicky Raftery
James Trickett
Alex Shuttes
Sarah Bright

and I'd like to thank them for involving me in a fascinating experience.

Hope you enjoy the book - sorry, didn't manage too much sex or horror in the end. Maybe next time.

P.H.

Other books by the same author available from
Crazy Horse Press:

'The Adventures of Stringy Simon'
ISBN 1 871870 07 0

'The Great Premium Bond Swizzle'
ISBN 1 871870 05 4

'The Day Trip'
ISBN 0 19 271510 0

Coming in 1999:

'The Willy Enlarging Elixir and Other Stories'

'Uncaging the Word'

PART 1: GOLDIE

Chapter 1

You have to choose your partners carefully with Kate Nantucket. Everyone's raving about her. She's the first singer since I don't know who that really gets to you even though you know your parents and all their friends like her. She's got all kinds of pain in her songs, the words are really deep, you can go on and on listening and still come up with something new - but they're also danceable. In fact they're a must at parties, you play them towards the end, when everyone's calmed down a bit. They're perfect for getting-off.

There's one of hers that everyone's got and I mean everyone, even the wimps know all the tracks, it's had a string of singles in the charts, they're all so different even though you can tell they came from the same album. They've all got that edge of sadness about them, even the dance tracks, no matter how hard you go at it you can't quite shake it out. That's why they're so good for getting-off I think, they always make you feel you really need each other, works every time. Like I say, you have to choose your partners carefully with Kate Nantucket.

There is just one other small reason why parents like her as well, apart from the words I mean. She's actually quite old. In fact she had a couple of hits in the late sixties, pathetic chewing-gum songs, they made her sing them like a first-former, old D.J.'s still play them.

After that she disappeared, didn't even get a 'where are they now' spot, and then in the last year it all happened at the same time. She was in Canada. She'd been living there for a few years, one reason why she hadn't been making the headlines probably, I mean keeping a Mountie's slippers warm isn't exactly big - when she was badly mugged, and lost, as well as her bag, cash, keys (they burgled her apartment), cards (they used them), and consciousness (she was in a coma for ten days), her baby. It would have been her first, even though she was in her thirties.

It doesn't seem right that success should come out of suffering - if it was me I'd always be thinking, if I could have known beforehand would I have chosen it or not? I'm sure most of them wouldn't. They must feel so guilty. Anyway, what she made wasn't a stack of songs about losing a baby, it was an album of the most fantastic love songs you have ever heard. The lyrics are brilliant, you can't help singing them. Sometimes they seem really old - not parent old, their songs were pathetic I think, how they've got the nerve to criticise ours I'll never know. I mean before-the-war old, sort of timeless; and sometimes they seem so modern, they tell you exactly how you'd want to be loved, even if you didn't know yourself. They come out of the belly of human experience, that's what Mr. Bowering told the fifth formers, or bowels, something down there anyway. They're doing them for G.C.S.E. English, thinks he's Joe Cool. He's not that cool though, Vlad's essay straightened him out.

Vlad's essay. One of *the* events of the decade. Who says words can't do any damage? It hit our place like a Scud missile. It was at times like that that you knew Mrs. Threadgold was a bit special, even though she didn't look very promising or sound it come to that, with her thin absolutely correct lady-like voice, and her fine down of silver hair. Like a dandelion clock, you could have blown her away - yet indomitable as royalty. Liz, my sister, she's married now, living in Leeds - met him at Uni - knew her before she got the headship and says she was just the same then. No-one took the mick or showed any disrespect even though she looked like a pushover. Goldie was the only nickname people used, and that's hardly offensive - quite nice actually, sort of affectionate. It wasn't as if she had any obvious signs of authority, I mean she didn't have a booming voice or anything, not even in Liz's day. Her authority seemed to have established itself years and years before, beyond all question, you simply knew not to challenge it. You knew it was real. If it wasn't for the fact we've talked about her so much recently, I'm sure I'd only have remembered the essay. Nothing else. I mean she didn't go round booming and drawing attention to herself, she was what you'd call quietly effective.

The essay came about from this thing they brought out with the G.C.S.E.: empathy. Daft really, everything you did you had to pretend you were there. 'So I said to Hitler....' That sort of thing, I ask you. 'Between us Florence and I were able to lift the poor fellow onto a makeshift bed and dress his wounds. He looked all but done in.' Bowering had us talking about Lord of the Flies - what's his name, William Golding, the one where the boys get stranded on the island. About how we could write different endings and so on. The chap gets a Nobel Prize and we change the ending, clever, or you could write a diary, 'After we smashed Simon's head in we decided to all calm down for a bit and get some sleep.' I'm not that keen on the book really, too violent. I prefer Coral Island. I don't see what's wrong with a bit of adventure.

Vlad put his hand up in that way of his when he's going to say something really devastating - he just puts it up and starts speaking never mind the rest of us, and leans back on the chair trying to fill the room with himself. He's so ignorant in some ways, just doesn't seem to be aware of other people and their feelings, his chat up lines are so tedious they wouldn't impress a second year. They don't in fact. But that's what makes him frightening when he comes up with an idea - you know once he's got it between his teeth he won't let it go for anyone. 'If you want to talk about realism,' he booms, 'let's talk about realism.' The class draws breath, we know the signs. And the signs are, when he quotes a teacher's own words back at him, he knows he can't be restrained because the teacher let him off the leash in the first place.

'I'll tell you why this book's no good,' he booms. It's now all of us against Bowering, we're sick of symbolism, tribal customs, and peering into the black and white undergrowth of the film. 'There's no *sex* for a start, I mean they're in a tropical island with half their clothes ripped off. How long were they there for God's sake?'

Bowering's voice goes to water. He's been 'engaging us in a dialogue' for three weeks, his expression for doing a set book, so now Vlad's dialoguing. 'Er well,' he says, promising start, 'we are talking about an English public school in the fifties...'

'Oh, ha, then why's the civil service riddled with *benders?*' That sort of thing, really milking the situation. 'They can't have been building shelters *all* the time, even you must realise that.'

'Um, you have to remember Golding's writing about the human *condition* as much as, er....' He's shipping water fast is Bowering.

'What about girls then, they're part of the human condition aren't they?' Vlad spreads his arm over the next chair, people don't usually sit next to him.

'Yes....of course....' He sneaks a look at his watch and realises he's going to make it to the bell. 'These are all things for you to consider when you plan your responses.'

'You want to try Terry Pratchett for a decent read, that's real imagination, there's no *fun* in this stuff, no-one laughs, except when they spear the pig up the arse, and that's not meant to be funny.' Golding wrote it, Sir read it out. Vlad knows when he's on safe ground.

But Bowser's packing away, ready for the serving-hatch ruck, staff versus sixth form, the rest of us have to queue. 'Remember,' he says, 'above all we have to reflect the *spirit* of the book....' Brrr. We're in the corridor.

Chapter 2

As you know, teachers carry a small 'Spotters' Guide to Kids' in the inside breast pocket next to their timetable and pay-slip, outlining the three main categories of child, with at-a-glance side and front view chart, male and female symbols for 100% error-free recognition - boffins who thank you for homework and bring presents when they get their 'A' levels, average kids who mess up the odd exercise but don't cause too much trouble, and thickies who fight and play up - plus main variations, sports heroes, special attention kids, regular assembly fainters, that sort of thing. But you won't find Vlad in there. He's intelligent *and* trouble. And I mean intelligent. And I mean trouble. When he grows up he'll expose Freemasonry, or corruption in the church. Or he'll be executed in Kuala Lumpur for drug-running. Whatever it is he'll be on the six o'clock news and there'll be support groups for him in places like Finland.

Vlad knows how people behave. He doesn't know much about his own behaviour, but he knows how other people behave. He's like a Silkworm missile, once he locks on to the heat of an engine its a gonner, too bad if it's one of yours not theirs, if you see what I mean. So when his essay came up at the Governors for discreet action, meaning a quiet suspension for improper behaviour, something like that, they found that he'd not only taken the precaution of photocopying it first - he'd had dozens done and was selling them round school like hot cakes. By the end of the week it's found its way into the local paper - '"A" LEVEL FILTH - A SIGN OF THINGS TO COME?' - and the Chairman of the Education Committee has to defend the new curriculum on the regional news.

That's Vlad. I don't do that many clever things, but do think I deserve a mention for managing to sell Vlad a copy of his own essay. It happened because mum's a teacher which means of course dad's a teacher, well, educational welfare to be exact, and all their friends are teachers.... ask me anything you like about dyslexia. SATS tests? Keystage 3? You get it all the time in our house, on the phone, in the kitchen, even up the garden, lady next door, retired deputy head. I can remember mum saying, 'Is there anything special you want for your thirteenth?' all coy, thinking I'd say a bra or something, some hopes, and I said straight away, a Walkman and some decent tapes. I just had to shut the education babble out it was driving me insane. It's bad enough wading through the pile of Times Educations in the back lobby whenever you want to get your wellies, teaching kids is a flipping *industry* I'm telling you. And mum's best friend- Mrs Price - Gloria - surprise surprise another teacher who also happens to be a governor at our place, which incidentally means they are sworn to secrecy about all the proceedings, came round the next evening and told mum everything, word for word, I didn't get a coffee all night, they kept shooing me out. And there on the side next morning, she must have left it, was wait for it a complete TYPED copy of the essay, not a word left out. I looked through it, it was all there, and I thought, how funny, they must have got some poor thing to type it all out and run off copies for the meeting. Who can it have been, not Miss

Parminger surely? It struck me as slightly ironic. I mean Andrea won a silver pen in the W.H. Smiths awards not twelve months ago but her essay wasn't typed and discussed at a governors' meeting. I slipped it into my bag, the sort of thing I very seldom do, and did some copies at the library.

Want to read it? You can have a choice, there's the governors' copy, which has been corrected, very thoughtful of them though it loses something in the translation I feel, or there's the original. I'll do the original. I'm warning you, it's gross.

*   *   *   *   *   *

No, I can't - I'll get banned or something. Tell you what, use the next couple of pages to write the most gross version of Lord of the Flies you can think of, then imagine something four times as bad. I mean it. That's Vlad's essay.

Chapter 3

Vlad. Talk about dramatic climax, the way the pilot died with a smile on his face was revolting, they didn't mistake *him* for a beast, that's for sure. I don't know how anyone can just sit there and write it down, not that Vlad minded too much obviously - in fact you could say it was inspired. I mean you see things on toilet doors but this is whole pages. I kept thinking about poor Miss Parminger having to type it. I wonder if she checked the spellings - now that's one t one s clitoris.... Bit different from the Chairman's report, committee with two t's, you've got to admit.

He ought to have his things chopped off never mind expulsion, he's sure to end up a rapist with a mind like that. But then what do I know. Old Parminger might have enjoyed it, maybe she got randy and passionate like the plain secretary always does in films when the chap manages to take off her glasses and hairgrips and suddenly you've got this raving temptress waiting to be ravaged. No, ravished. I don't know enough about people that's half my trouble. Some of the third years actually clubbed together to try and persuade him to write a sequel, forty p and a Twix I suppose that's what you call a writer's advance.

Governors' meetings aren't what they used to be, take my word for it. Mum says she didn't even know school governors *existed* in her day and she wanted to be a teacher from the age of five months - one of those vile kids that hangs round the staffroom all day looking for jobs, 'Miss shall I take your dinner plates back for you,' that sort, probably used to lick her thumb after just for a taste of the gravy. And that sort doesn't miss much I can tell you, they can't wait to get into an empty staffroom and read the notices, God help you if you've got any problems. '*ALL STAFF PLEASE NOTE: The parents of Jenny Pinkerton YEAR EIGHT have been having SEVERE PROBLEMS recently following Mr Pinkerton's COURT APPEARANCE FOR SHOPLIFTING AND OTHER OFFENCES. Things have improved slightly since last week's ORDER OF RESTRAINT limiting the father's access, but if Jenny should show any signs of stress such as FREQUENT NEED TO VISIT THE TOILET, please deal with her sympathetically.*' Imagine it.

She's got big hopes I'll turn out to be one, mum has - teacher not governor - she doesn't say anything blatant she's not that daft, it's just the way these little pointed comments and hints come out whenever she's got me trapped in the kitchen or somewhere.

Funny how Liz didn't have to put up with it, too clever that's why, jammy devil, but I'm your ideal candidate, Set 2, polite, does what she's told, homework in on time, God stop, stop, I can't take anymore. There's just ONE reason why I don't come straight out and tell her no thanks I'm not interested. And that's Brendan. Brendan Price. Mrs Brendan Price, God, if only. He's so sexy my mouth goes dry. It has now. He's the Head Boy. All the others on the commemoration plaque have got such pathetic names, creep after creep going back to 1927 or something like that. But his is perfect. BRENDAN PRICE. It's in the brightest lettering too, as if they knew somehow.

He wants to be one.

He also happens by chance (ah God) to be mum's friend's son - the one who told her about the meeting and left the essay. If it wasn't for that he wouldn't even know I existed, not that he does really not as an individual, a young WOMAN, he still thinks I'm about five like I was when I used to follow him round our house with a Ladybird book and a runny nose. But I'm working on it. Quietly. I'm what you call hanging in there, biding my time. I mean I'm not sensational looking, not like Melissa, lucky cow, he's already noticed her, or some of his friends have anyway they're like predators honestly, sixth formers. But there are just two little possibilities I'm hanging my hat on. One is he might turn out to like the kind of steady sort - not that he does at the moment, he's after the new girl from the convent, the busty one, spotted her pretty quick, but he *might,* in time - the other is, you never know but sometimes quite plain girls become unbelievable pin-ups over night, I've seen it happen, and boys that used to act like they were a pane of glass in need of a window cleaner are suddenly all over them. You never know. So I'm kind of keeping in touch the best I can. I can baby-sit now, and she's asked me a couple of times, not when he's there of course, worst luck. I reckon I've got about twelve months before his sis refuses to be baby-sat anymore. He'll be off to college then, probably, so I'd better get growing quick. I wish there were hormone pills or something.

Anyway, what was it before Brendan dragged me off and seduced me, oh yes the meeting. The famous essay.

He got away with it. Absolutely scott-free, not even a telling-off. And the one who apparently got him off the hook was, you've guessed it, Goldie herself. Gospel according to mum, direct from Mrs. Price. Goldie on Golding: she said he was dull and sexist, more or less what Vlad said come to think of it, and deserved anything that came his way. Not only that, but she would have passed the essay as well.

HAH! I can just picture her. She was so quiet and utterly unflappable, there was no answering her I remember quite clearly now. She was completely sincere. Mum talked about her endlessly, I think she kind of idolised her. Which was how I knew she was dying, not that it was a secret. Everyone knew. They tried to retire her at one stage, but there was no chance, she wasn't going to be shoved off to the sidelines before she was ready. Illness isn't a crime.

Chapter 4

I don't know if you've noticed this at all, but schools are very desk-bound places. I mean the ideal student is one with her bum perched firmly on a seat and a pen in her hand. I remember when they were dancing on the Berlin wall, we'd just started German, I mean my parents were practically in tears, they just sat there in front of the telly gob-smacked. And I could feel it too, it was impossible to just sit there without being aware an irreversible change was taking place on the earth's surface - like a new continent emerging out of the Atlantic, something that big. The day after, I went off thinking, they'll send out a party with garlands and messages of support, they'll bring back a piece of the wall - *the* wall - and ceremonially place it under glass in front of the whole school as a source of inspiration. Goldie would have seen to that, I know she would, that was the kind of thing she did, that was how she was different. The world came first with her, not school. It's not that we don't ever go on trips or anything - we do. Geography field trip, visit to the R.S.C., week's work experience, you can almost see them quailing in case we pick up some kind of social MALAISE in the big wide world and get deflowered of our classroom-virginity, Alton Towers for the highest attenders, skiing if you can afford it. It's just that they're never spontaneous. Never. I know you've got to plan and send out letters and all the rest, but you can't always expect man's destiny to give you a term's notice can you?

That was what Goldie understood. Her classroom was the world. Except it happened to be the time of her first long absence, when they took her in for tests and kept her.

So we trooped in the day after and it was 'Have you got a note', 'Turn to page so-and-so', 'No you may not go to the toilet', the same as any other day.

At the same time world history was being reshaped for ever they were telling Mrs. Threadgold she had a few more months to live. But she was remembered in our prayers, in fairness. No mention in lessons, no visits, but her terminal illness fell conveniently for our prayers.

*　　*　　*　　*　　*　　*

Apart from mum and his mum being friends, the only reason Brendan knows I exist is thanks to Mrs. Threadgold. He's head boy, Brendan is, I don't know if I've mentioned it already, but he is. Which shows how intelligent and popular with the teachers he is, as well as spunky. In some schools the head boy and girl make a thank-you speech on prize-giving night, give the main guest a bouquet, and that's about it. It's awesomely sickly when you think about it, the 'speech' is written for them and vetted, what do they think they're going to say, piss off and don't come back or something? How would they know in advance anyway, the speaker could turn out to be alright. But if he isn't, or she, they get the same tacky vote of thanks and flowers anyway chosen by the secretary. 'Thank you for your lucid and erudite and ahem stimulating words, which I'm sure gave all present much food for thought.' In fact sitting in plastic seats through your average speech night is my idea of hell. And I mean *we're* used to it, we get it all day, god knows what it must be like for the parents poor devils. My backside gets so numb some days it spreads halfway up my spine, which is why the words pain in the arse mean something special for a school pupil.

But at our place it's always been the head boy or girl's job to choose a community scheme for the school to be involved in. And I'm not talking about a guide dog for the blind tin in the main foyer either, they really have to get stuck in and get us involved. It's their job, but it's their privilege as well, because they have absolute freedom of choice. Goldie always backed it without question. Liz was head girl when she was there, I'll never make it in a fit. She declared the school a nuclear free zone, and they had all the headed notepaper over-printed. Can you imagine that?, *'Dear Sir/Madam, your son/daughter is required to serve a detention of .... minutes at.....pm on ....., 199-, for the following reason........ THIS IS A NUCLEAR-FREE AREA SAY NO TO RADIOACTIVE WASTE Please sign acknowledgement slip below and return to form teacher by.....Yours sincerely..... CHADWELL LANE HIGH SUPPORTS LOW COMBUSTION ENERGY RESEARCH PROJECTS'*

They had an eventful year I believe and caused a bit of a stir, which would have suited Goldie down to the ground the crafty so and so. There was no way she was going to let world events slip by on the BBC while there was life in her body.

Some people said Brendan's idea was a bit tame. I suppose it was in a way, I mean it's hard to follow Terence Higgins Trust Year, Child Abuse Awareness and Rainforest Relief, those are the three we've had since I started there. Would you believe we actually own twenty four acres of Brazil? We do. It would be brilliant to set up a half-term activity centre there I think, mind I'm not sure it would be very fair on the food chains us barging in every twelve weeks, might give the poor pitcher plants hiccups. No, I'm only joking, it's great we saved it from being chopped down.

Which is why Brendan's idea to stop them building a Humbolt's D.I.Y. place on Turner's Meadow took a while to catch on. It's not everyone's idea of a crusade to save the planet, I know, I mean it must seem a bit *microscopic* after campaigning to save thousand-year-old hardwoods. But we can't all go charging off to the southern hemisphere can we? Sometimes you just have to sit in a puddle among the pram-frames and tyres and count water-fleas. Otherwise they'll dig it up.

Chapter 5

The Memorial Service. We elected someone from each form to go and they closed the school. It wasn't exactly a vote, not in our case anyway, just a couple of us offering and settling it between us. You don't need votes when you've got respect.

So I went and so did Liz, she took a couple of days off lectures and came down. There were a lot of them there, former pupils who had taken it on themselves to make a kind of journey of homage, it was beautiful, you never see generations rubbing shoulders like that. You might think you do, at a wedding or a big christmas, say, but they're not really together, they've all got something different in mind, someone's in charge telling them when it's time for this or that. They make an effort for the occasion.

This was different. It wasn't quiet or desperately solemn, a lot of them were talking while they waited: but there was a kind of stillness about everyone. There was no pointless movement, no scratching or sudden turning round nothing at all, nothing - I've not thought of it this way - nothing that suggested people wanted to be somewhere else. No agitation.

Something else. I didn't get my mind round it straight away, because the room we came into, it was part of the Guildhall, I've only been in the main section where they hold the operatics and so on, had arched windows and thick battlement-type stone walls, and as we came in, there was an almost shabbily dressed man playing the piano, playing it so you felt you were inside it, you know - when the nape of your neck tingles - kind of fills you inside and out till you get the feeling you're actually in there with the hammers and the wires. There was that and the windows, the ivy outside and a soft rain, and there was the table with a honey coloured candle, sandalwood or whatever, big, the flame almost afloat in its wax, where the tributes were placed: flowers, but odd things too, books, an ornamental plate, pieces of weathered wood, a pouch of some kind with something heavy in it, could have been money - each thing unique and particular, lovingly placed down: there was something almost ancient about it, like death is a journey your loved ones prepare you for, a going on alone.

A kind of awareness started to come over me, that this was not going to be easy. It wasn't going to be a turn your back on the deceased and clear off service, you know? The room filled, and changed shape. Chairs materialised behind the covered table so it was no longer at the front, more in the middle. The formality of seating was broken down, but it only brought you closer to the real formality, a kind of dignity in the room, the more the rows got ruptured the more aware of it you were, they brought it in with them and nothing could undo it.

There were people I knew, and people I recognised but didn't know, had seen in the local media. Not just local - I think our M.P. was there, for example. But whatever new shapes the chairs made or unmade, without moving at all the figure of Mr. Threadgold was always the natural centre. People moved, but the respect stayed on him, a lovely shaggy, strong featured, loose shouldered old man alone in his pride and sadness.

I don't know, I know nothing. One thing I found out in that stone-walled room where people stood so completely together you couldn't see a seam, the ivy on the sills greened silently by a drifting soft rain, a thing I'll never ever forget. You can only die properly without God.

Instead, a man spoke the names of history, Atlee, Bertrand Russell, Rudolph Steiner so unemphatically in her memory, I knew for the first time the history of the race and the living memory of anyone in it, no matter who, is one. There was no altar, no kneeling and imploring, just a saying and a listening of such breathtaking quiet it will never leave me, not if I live to be a mother wading through nappies and cough-juice, not if I live to be ninety and curled over a stick.

I thought you had to 'know' a man to grow up, like Jo, we hang on her every word because she had Kev after the youth club, I bet she felt nothing - but what you have to know is death. I thought I did. I'd seen hearses and cats in the road, but that wasn't it. Death doesn't pass you by.

But now I know this. Tele's glass and bits, and Heaven's a drug. They numb you. They sever you from your losses and you are no-one. In her passing Goldie left me that. She was an atheist. She kept it from us all that time, but shared it at the last. It was her legacy.

There was a woman at her husband's side, tall, weathered, you could prick the sadness. Another face, I knew, not local. She moved into the silence, and sang. We knew the song, but it was so beautiful I heard it for the first time and welled up and cried.

The rumour was true. Kate Nantucket. Goldie's daughter.

PART 2: THE FORGE

Chapter 6

GROOGH! Exams.

Do you have a favourite word? I know, don't tell me - boy, sex, kiss, date, Friday night, put your books away. I mean do you have a favourite *sounding* word. It's a little game Bowering plays with us if the lesson finishes early, can't have our growing minds lying dormant while there's two minutes of enriching English time to cram them with. Whoever it was crammed his crammed it with something rich and fertile that's for sure. Horse manure I'd say, at a rough guess. No, that's not fair, it's a good game, our books are full of words like delphinium, graciously and suchlike. I keep changing mine. Elbow I like, that's a good one. Vlad chose basking shark, clever. Conundrum. That's another one I like, but my top word of the moment is GROOGH. I love it. Like in old comics when the colonel takes a swig of wood veneer by mistake instead of his tea, spits it out in a plume of spray over the visiting general and his wife and yells, GROOGH. They make me die, words like that. Arf is another one. A kind of ball-shaped mongrel with eyebrows and a black nose, sees a string of sausages trailing from the butcher's boy's bike and chases after it. ARF ARF ARF. They crack me up.

Actually, they're not so bad, Bowering's lessons, he does try, I must say that - sometimes you wish he wouldn't try quite so hard, but at least he does try. He's got us doing these problem page letters at the moment, thinks its *relevant*. Now there's a vile-sounding word if you want one. Relevant. I get this image of a maths teacher standing in front of his class in motor cycle leathers.

Anyway, Bowering obviously thinks we spend all day reading the problem letters in Just Seventeen so he's got to have a bit of it - well we do but that's not the point - so he's gone to Smiths and bought a few copies, imagine the till-girl: 'Shall I wrap them sir, would sir like a receipt?', and cut out the problems and given them to us to discuss in groups. Except Janey. Janey's a high-flier with problems, I'd say she's probably in the gifted category, she doesn't feel the need to discuss them, she just sees one and bangs off an answer, it's phenomenal. There we all are weighing them up and arguing the odds and Janey's on her fourteenth. She goes up to Bowering, 'Can I have some more?', he's rummaging desperately in his bag he's already spent half his wages, thought they'd last him a term or more. She's the Oliver Twist of the letters pages, is Janey, she laps them up. He's got her making up her own now, I've seen some of them, not many mind, she writes that fast she's over the page before you can catch up.

She's got the knack, you've got to hand it to her. They all start the same way, with a little heading, there are dozens of them. *'BEING BRIBED. I am a 12 year old girl....'* there's no 'Dear Patsy' or any of that nonsense, you get 100% square deal problem with Janey. *'I am a 12 year old girl and I am being bribed by my brother because I've been smoking with my friends and he know's about it. My mum and dad are going on a weekend away somewhere and he says his going to have sex with me if I don't stop smoking. I am so scared I can't tell anybody also I think I am pregnant.'*

Now that's a hell of a problem. I mean it would take our table a fortnight to decide which bit to tackle first. Not Janey. There's none of that weighing-up lark for her. *'Go and visit your local doctor and don't worry about your parents he won't tell them you have been smoking if you ask him not to also he will help you give them up but you have to be sure you want to first.'*

That's Janey for you, you have to be up early to get one past her. She's to teenage trouble what Col. Saunders is to the chickens. Sometimes she's so good she gets the problem and the advice all in one.

'I'M TO FAT. I'm a girl of 13 and I have a really good appitite but the problem is when I go to school people say oh your fat and sometimes I really get mad and cry and say not every one can be slime. Also people say you will never get a boyfriend but lots of fat people get boyfriends its not what you look like its your personality that counts.'

She's done pages of them. Her book won't lie flat, it kind of expands like a bellows at rest. They run into one another, the way wet leaves in the gutter do, and block the drains.

She's actually caused the odd problem or two herself, has Janey, bossing the library users. Volunteered in the first year, before they caught on what a right pain she can be if she's let off the leash. I've spent a few lunch-hours in there myself and I'm telling you she runs the show, you daren't sniff.

There was only one problem that ever floored her. I'm afraid I'm a bit of a tease sometimes, and it wasn't the best kept secret in the world that she had a bit of a soft spot for old Brendan. So I slipped one across to her one lesson. *'Dear Janey, my problem is I have a friend who is rather keen on the HEAD BOY at our school but she is petrified to approach him in case he says no. What should she do? A well wisher.'*

Poor old Janey. If she'd have known I go weak at the sound of his name she could have wiped the floor with me. But instead she went like a fiery furnace and hid her face till the buzzer. It was the only time anyone ever stopped her.

I won't do it again, though.

Anyway, we're in one of these lessons, it's a typical Bowering lesson: J17s everywhere with little windows where the problems have been cut out, some of us just sitting reading them, there's a big group 'discussing' which means making up unprintable answers, occasionally huddling in to slag off someone in another class, Bowering's with the quiet group - 'Yes, but on the other hand, couldn't you say...?', he's broadening their outlook, they're riveted, you can see them wiping away the yawns on their sleeves - and Janey's on her own beavering away at a small pile stacked beside her, when there's a knock on the door and in walks a gaggle of Very Important Persons, led by Mr Dooley done up in his Sunday best you've never seen anything like it, he's got a bow-tie on. Looks like that horoscope chap, Russell Grant.

I used to like Mr. Dooley, he was this sweet old deputy head who took us for history in the first year, thought girls were precious, fragile little things, obviously hadn't seen Laura Kenealy on the rampage, he lined us up in separate lines and sat us in separate rows nearest the heaters. You could actually tell by the tone of his voice whether he was talking to a boy or a girl, assuming you hadn't noticed he called us by our christian names, that is. Probably would have had us back in pinnies, if it wasn't for Brussels. I used to love those lessons, it was like going into another world.

Now the governors have gone and breathed life into him and set him off again, they've put him in charge, Acting Headmaster, till they can decide on Goldie's replacement. It's not fair. I don't want to think unkindly of him, I want to remember him how he was.

Bowering automatically starts to rise from his seat, funny how teachers do that, like bubbles stuck to the bottom, always ready to lift off at a moment's notice. I don't think it's natural. They set too much store by obedience. 'Don't get up Mr. Bowering,' says old Dooley wagging him down like the conductor of the London Philharmonic, he's loving every minute of it. 'You don't mind if we just *perambulate* for a minute or two, we won't disturb you.....' He gets a bit of the old vocab in, just to let Bowers know *he* was taught English the proper way, solid, copper-bottomed sound practice, not like the flimsy stuff that passes for education nowadays. And so on, it's all there.

It's good to be in the know sometimes. Having a school governor who comes round and twits to mum till the small hours does have its up side. For example, I'm the only one in the room, only pupil anyway, who knows that Dooley's not in charge of this little excursion at all, it's actually Hearnshaw the one with his hand still on the door knob squirming with embarrassment. They're candidates for Goldie's job. Today's the interview day for the headship. Hearnshaw's a young senior teacher, they're sort of dogsbodies that get to run uniform checks, supervise detention, that sort of thing. They're not important enough to be on interviewing panels, but they get to show the candidates around. They're kind of like bullets in a gun I always think, senior teachers, sort of lying there in the breech, waiting to be shot to the top when the trigger gets pulled.

Normally Hearnshaw might get quite a buzz out of this, lording it over a bevy of future heads including his eventual boss, but sadly for him Dooley's stolen the show, he thought glory had passed him by, but here he is all of a sudden, the sitting tenant and favourite to get the job, and he's damn well going to make sure the others know it.

He breaks from the group and strolls over to Janey as if he owns the place. 'This looks mighty interesting,' he fingers the old bow-tie, can't believe he's top dog. 'Tell us what you've been doing....' He's figured that one girl on her own is a safer bet than a group of friends sitting together, but he's figured wrong.

She looks up, swimming with nerves.

'A....ah, problems.... Good. Good. Read one out for us....' If he wasn't feeling so full of himself, Dooley would have noticed the magazines scattered around and taken a bit more care, but he's totally in role, hands clasped across his paunch waiting for the 'problem' - probably thinks it's a grammar check or something, might give him the opportunity to get one over on the others and pass us a few tips.

Her voice wavers slightly. Dooley cocks his head to one side like an owl that's spotted game, the way he used to when we were first years and made up to him by lisping in tiny voices. *'FALLING IN LOVE.'* She's fine once she starts, the problem takes over. *'I am a 15 year old girl and I am falling in love with this boy in my set he pinches my bottom and sometimes smiles at me. He also makes me laugh mind you anyone can make me laugh books make me laugh but sometimes this boy really gets up my noise. Like green runy snot. He gets on my nerves sometimes.... WORRIED ABOUT MY PERIOD...'* She's in full flight now, she's even putting on a voice, like the 'Points of View' lady. *'WORRIED ABOUT MY PERIOD. I am so worried about my period because I haven't started yet and I am 15 and I want to have sex with this boy but I don't know whether I can or not. All the other girls in my class say....'*

'I *don't* think' his voice cracks out like a rifle shot, 'we need hear any more.' He scowls at Bowering.

35

You'll keep till I've got my feet firmly under the table, that kind of scowl. 'I expect this kind of thing makes the occasional pleasant change from your *proper* work. Thank you.'

He's lost the initiative though, and the others come out from their cover and begin to go round the tables.

Reminds me of the story about the man in the village, old Dooley does - he goes to the headman and says, 'I've got to have a bigger hut, there are too many of us, it's driving me mad.' And the headman says, 'The answer is simple my fine brave, get yourself a goat and keep it by you for company.' So the man brings home a goat and crams it into the hut with his family. But, instead of getting better things get worse, so he goes back to the headman and the headman says. 'The answer is simple my fine brave, the goat must go.' And the goat is bled and put in the pot and everyone has room to sleep well for the first time, and when he next sees the headman the man falls at his feet in gratitude.

Nice story. Well we're the family and Dooley's the goat, and he's not going anywhere.

Old Bowering just sits there gobsmacked by the whole thing. He watches the candidates tiptoeing round the chairs, I don't think I've ever seen him so stuck for words before. Come to think of it he's probably peeing himself in case there's a repeat performance in front of the governors, 'MORE FILTH

AT CHADWELL LANE' - like there was with Vlad, who incidentally has wagged it today, he's probably picking his toenails right this minute in front of Sesame Street.

Wonder what old Parminger would make of 'Worried About My Period'?

One of the candidates comes and perches on a branch by us, settling her feathers for a long stay. Her radar's already picked me out as the neurotically polite one who won't show her up whatever happens, I hate it when people twig you straight away like that. 'Do you enjoy your English lessons, my dear,' she says, fixing me with these little beady black intensely interested eyes. 'My dear?' PARDON? What kind of cupboard's she been locked away in for the last fifty years. I can't believe it. I go bright red, something I hate, HATE happening. I could run out of the room with embarrassment, but instead I just stare up at her like a complete moron and the words won't come. She's like something out of the catalogue, she's wearing these lovely swishy jade green culottes, black low-heeled shoes, cream blouse with a bit of edging, burgundy coat (shoulder pads), brooch. Her hair catches the light as she turns, it's cut quite high at the back, so neat you could put a pencil line round it. It shimmers. Her eyes bore in on me for an answer and the look on her face says, Interest, Interest, Care, Concern, she's like a perfectly manicured NAIL, she's got me mesmerised, I'm dumb.

'Kay...?' It's Bowering, Mister Bowering, sorry, you know who your friends are at times like this. He says my name quietly and I know where I am again, it breaks the spell. I mumble an answer and she wafts away while she's still ahead thank God.

They seem to be giving Janey a wide berth, sensible. There's an insurance-clerk kind of chap, light-weight suit, glasses with a straight edge at the top - everything about him says 'I don't want to offend anyone' in a loud and clear voice, I dislike people like that, they can be quite spiteful in my experience, once they're sure no-one's looking. He's run into a bit of turbulence at the card-sharps' table by the look of it, there's a bit of laughter which he's joined in with, but he's not looking too comfortable. His eyes are looking for a bolt-hole.

The one who does look at ease has found the spare chair next to Janey, so I was wrong. He's got his legs sprawled out as if he's intending to stay, and he's thumbing through a J17 with what looks like a certain familiarity. 'My daughter reads this,' he says casually, elbow on the table. His voice is warm and confident. He's got Janey on side at least, she's rabbiting away now, he'll be there for weeks.

We're just about to start clearing up our pile of cuttings when the girl next to me gives me a socking great elbow in the side and thrusts her eyes at the floor near Janey, urgently. There must be a doggy-do down there, or at least a pound coin the way she's looking. And then I see it. It's important alright. The chap by Janey. He's got Fido Dido socks.

Chapter 7

As I was saying: exams - yuk. Or GROOGH. They were kind of indefinitely postponed when Goldie died and everyone thought they might just forget about them this time round. But they haven't. Dear old Dooley announced it this morning.

I've never done this before in my life, but I'm thinking of having a small bet. There's this boy in our class, he's such a wreck, Paul - he's so critically gorgeous actually, he's got pale blue brilliantly humorous eyes, they say 'smile' the whole time, no matter what, and lovely tousled blond hair that makes him look as if he's just escaped a lynch mob trying to string him up for bedding the sheriff's wife. You can't take him seriously, he's got 'waster' written all over his forehead, but if you ever did he'd take you for such a hiding. Half the school would drop their knickers for him if he so much as looked in their direction, but the only girl he's ever been interested in is lady luck - he's besotted: she treats him like dirt, but it only makes him crave for her more. He's your twenty-four carat genuine article, the school addictive gambler. He's like the Sundance, he really hasn't got a clue he's so good-looking - well he has in a way, it's so obvious how the girls make up to him you'd have a job to miss it, but it doesn't seem to signify. If he got two aces in a hand of cards and he needed a third his eyes would bore through the pack with desire, but if the best looking girl in the class threw herself at his feet, which she virtually has done, he would just respond in that kind of half-aware way you stroke a cat that brushes your legs, and get on with his game.

Nothing arouses him from the kind of amicable trance he goes round the school in except a game of cards or a bet. He's always got two or three packs on him, they come out of his pockets the same way other people reach for a comb or a pen, only more often. He just sits there quietly shuffling them in lessons, like a comforter, I think he'd be in difficulties if he forgot to bring them except it wouldn't happen, any more than you'd forget your shoes, they're part of his clothing. I don't think he's got a single enemy, he's not really aware enough of people to be nasty to them, but his only friends, well, partners, are the card school, they talk his language. They have four that I know of, maybe more, places around the school where they can play undisturbed, all warm, quiet and completely out of sight. They can actually play for hours at a time in almost complete silence, in fact they don't like talking, it spoils their concentration. I've never seen them in session of course, they don't go in for audiences, but I've seen them right at the end of term when the teachers *let* you play cards. They're amazing, they can't play for fun, they don't know how. Everyone else is bragging away, arguing, showing their hands to onlookers, taking and giving advice on what to play next, and they're over in a corner firing cards into the middle, shuffling, redealing, almost in a trance. Like lions at a kill.

He had the odds worked out for every subject, before they even announced the exams. He's a very systematic person Paul is, at heart, I'm sure the teachers would die if they realised how genned up he was on kids' academic records. He could give a complete print-out on any pupil, any year: exam record, classwork, homework, any discipline problems, illness, absence, extenuating circumstances - move of house, bereavement, separation. It's a cruel business, laying odds, you can't afford to be sentimental. My parents get told bull from start to finish of every parent night - sorry, 'consultation evening' - but if they could only set Paul up with a small desk in the corner somewhere he'd give a complete academic rating for any pupil in seconds. My odds haven't changed much since the first year, I can still get between 12-1 and 20-1 against coming top in most subjects except French (33-1, but that's because of Claudia, she always gets a hundred per cent, her dad's French. She actually marked one set of papers last year. In fact, if you wanted to make a killing, you'd spike her morning Pepsi and put a stack on Laura Hamilton at the last minute, but knowing Paul he'd call the bets off. He's no fool.). The only one that has changed is English, 7-1 the pig, he's noticed I'm improving. I am too, I feel more confident now we're doing set books, that's because I'm a bit of a reader, I don't just rely on the videos like everyone else. Videos are OK, they help you remember the story, but they don't always tell you what's going on inside people's heads, and they certainly don't tell you what's going on inside the author's head. You've got to read it to find that out. I mean Tess gets raped in the woods and everyone's craning their necks to catch a glimpse of their bits and pieces in between the tastefully filmed interplay of light and dark and all that - it doesn't exactly compel you to contemplate finer points, does it? I don't care what Bowering thinks, he's not that good.

The reason why I fancy my chances this year is because it's not a proper exam. There's no question paper - you have to work out a topic, plan it all out beforehand so Bowering can check it, then you write it up in the exam and hand it in. I think I'll do alright at that. It's proper exams I can't handle, when you don't know what's going to come up, I just turn the paper over and freeze, even if I've revised the right questions. It always happens. The thing is, I've got a really brilliant idea for a topic - it's going to take a bit of writing but I'm sure I can do it. You don't even lose marks for not finishing, they grade you then you carry on with it in term time. It's right up my street.

There's only one problem. Vlad. Vlad can write. There's a good chance he'll do something daft and come last. There's a fair chance he'll stay in bed for the week and not turn up at all. You never know with Vlad. But if he shows up and he's on song it's no contest. He can write like a script-writer, he can just turn it out. He's 3-1.

I suppose I could have an each-way and maybe win a few pence, but I don't want to do that. If I'm going to bet on myself I'm going to have a decent bet, then I'll have something to crow about if I come up. Come top. I think I might.

Chapter 8

I get in and dump my bag. There's no homework but we've all got tons of revision of course. I'd rather have homework actually, at least you know where to start and finish. I'm about to take the stairs - I always get the straight-jacket off as soon as I come in, and put something old and baggy on - when the kitchen door opens, or quarter opens. Mum. 'Nice day then...?' What? What's she up to, I usually get at least a half-hour winge about reading schemes, parents' ignorance and stress straight out. She must be having an affair, no, not in that outfit. She beckons me over, the door opens further, and what have we here, oh God no, Mrs. Price, I'm in the web like it or not.

My heart always skips a beat when I see her, I can't get rid of this kind of half-feeling she'll have Brendan in tow, he'll formally propose in front of both sets of parents, we'll pop the champagne and the two houses will become one. Mind, it skips it fairly quickly, he wouldn't be seen dead with her, in fact if there's one racing certainty in life it's that Brendan won't be found anywhere near his mum, and who can blame him, she's so beaky and busybodyish, one of these awful people who asks you how you are and listens intently to your answer, I never feel at ease with her. What a way to talk about your future mother-in-law, touch wood. I touch the sideboard, formica actually, and mum immediately starts pouring, thinks I'm demanding tea, blimey, she *is* distracted.

'How was your day then?' Brendan's mum, great toucan's beak of a nose bearing in on me waiting for an answer. I dunk a biscuit really deep hoping to cause a diversion - mum hates it - but she takes no notice.

'Alright,' I slurp my wet biscuit before it keels over and drops off. 'How was yours?'

'Oh *we've* had a lovely day,' she beams secretively at mum. 'We've been going through the CV's of the candidates for Mrs. Threadgold's job.... Did you catch a *glimpse* of any of them in school?'

Yuk. (GROOGH.) So that's it, she's after the lowdown on the candidates. Yes mum, so you should be embarrassed, you're like a pair of vultures. Nevertheless, if you've got influence, use it I say, so I give her a quick run-down, and I mean run-down, leaving her in no doubt what hopeless cases they are, except old Fido Dido of course, who I leave till last then praise up a bit, like estate agents do when they've got a house they want to sell you. Not mentioning his socks of course, I'm not completely daft. When adults ask kids their opinion, you have to be careful never to show more than a very grudging approval for something you like. Anything approaching enthusiasm gets them suspicious. Besides, what's there to get carried away about, there'll never be anyone like Goldie again, god I miss her sometimes. Half the things I miss I didn't even know mattered at the time. I mean I thought assemblies were boring, for one thing. They are boring. But they were brisk and boring before, they were upbeat I suppose, sort of businesslike. Goldie always had a bit of go about her. She was ancient, but she got on with things, left you feeling time was important, there was lots to cram in. Now they're solid granite boring, they really are heavy, every prayer is like a ton weight.

I lug my bag upstairs and try to make a start on the revision. If you're going to do it you might as well start early before the nausea builds up, then you can reward yourself with a couple of hours telly at the end.

But I can't face it. As I stare at the books they get bigger and heavier, and turn to stone. They lie there like ruddy paving slabs, and won't open themselves. *'Dear Janey, my problem is revision. I want to pass, but the books won't open, and when they do they're written in Sanskrit anyway and don't make any sense to me. Please help, I'm going under.'* I wonder what she'd say.

'Dear Going-Under. I don't know what your getting so worked up about. Your not thinking of becoming a teacher are you? Forget it, there the most boring people on earth. Just start on your favourate subject and leave the others for now, the books might open theirselfs up later when your in a better mood. Good luck.'

Quite right Janey, I knew you'd sort it for me. I clear the tombstones off my table, get out my English things, and before I know it I'm wandering the landscapes of my project, lost to the world. You'd better be on your best form Vlad this is going to be hot stuff.

Chapter 9

You know you're ancient the day you discover that first-years don't know what chalk is. It's true. They've never had the experience of listening to a stick of chalk tap, squeak and scrape its way down a pock-marked greying board while the teacher drones at you over his right shoulder. I miss it, I do. You knew you were in a school when you passed those fans of board-rubber marks on the outside wall of every entrance, and the class clown smeared his hand from the gully of dust and went round smacking the backs of blazers with it. First years these days, they've lost touch with all the traditions, you see them strolling around discussing profiling forms and career options, they think schools are places of learning.

As a matter of fact, that reminds me, next time you hear me going on about dear old sweet old Mr. Dooley, just pinch me will you. He's got the most vicious temper when things go wrong. You go weeks without a hint of it, then suddenly he blows like a volcano, face all fiery red, eyes bulging, usually at some group of boys who've decided to get his rag up. He's fine when the girls keep smiling and the boys keep quiet, and everyone does what they're told, then he can play the old village schoolmaster and fount of wisdom to his heart's content. It works best with first and second years. You don't learn a fat lot, except how to keep him in role for forty minutes and make life easy for yourself.

Rumour has it that in the days of chalk and blackboards he kept a slipper in his desk. When a boy misbehaved (I don't know what he did about girls, made them wash the staff coffee cups probably) when a boy misbehaved he would have him over a chair at the front and slipper him. The special little Dooley version of this was that he had a number chalked, in reverse, on the slipper sole - the number of boys he'd slippered from the start of his career. So when it was your turn, as well as a sore backside you'd have 1008, or whatever it was, branded right way round on the seat of your trousers.

I don't know whether that's true, but I've heard it a couple of times from different people. I've also heard that he didn't used to blow his stack in those days, just calmly changed the number on the shoe while the victim slunk back to his seat, and then carried on with the lesson.

Funny, his old classroom still exists, in fact it's still sometimes used for lessons, like one of those Victorian working museums where you go to watch them making peppermint humbugs and candles. We call it the Forge. It has got a number, but only the new teachers use it. Everyone else calls it the Forge. It's completely detached from everywhere else in the place, over by the netball court - it's got iron window frames, desks that haven't seen the light of day for twenty years - the cuts and carvings go down a couple of inches now - great concertina radiators with a dozen coats of paint on them baking slowly all winter, and of course a blackboard on an easel which you raise and lower by pegs attached to little chains so they don't get lost or pinched. At nights and weekends the door is padlocked.

It *was* joined on to the rest once, well, joined on to the metalwork room anyway, but that got knocked down for the netball court, they cut plastic sheets in labs now instead - so it stands quietly on its own like a shrine to days gone by. It's a perfect haunt for bullies, snoggers and smokers.

And gamblers. It's one of Paul's little dens, he's won and lost fortunes there. It's also the place to go if you want to lay a bet on any event in the school calendar you can think of. He actually sits there, can you believe it, like a lord in residence two or three mornings a week, just collecting in, paying out, laying odds on anything you care to name - house tournaments, football teams, swimming galas, head boy, head girl, prefects, detentions, suspensions, expulsions, prize winners, runners up, exam placings, classes, sets: you could lay a bet on who's going to get pregnant if you wanted, teacher or pupil, and the sex of the baby; you could bet on a couple of kids having a fight, they often do. He sits there bold as brass, odds chalked up on the board, always changing, always following the ebb and flow of money. All the sixth form know, they're his biggest customers though so it's kept in the family if you know what I mean. It's the biggest open secret in the school.

Actually, we're not all raving gamblers: most people don't go there to bet, they wouldn't be so daft, they go there just to hang around, to sniff the air and get the feel of things. Everything that happens hits the Forge first. If you bust up with your boyfriend you can find out what your chances of getting back together are before you know yourself. It's that kind of place. It's the place to be. And of course when exams come round that's where you head for the minute you get through the gates. Whole year groups mill round, you can't move for people. It's like the Great Barrier Reef - all the different shoals mingling together, all darting for coral at the sniff of member of staff, re-emerging as soon as the shadow passes. I wouldn't miss it for anything. You don't know you've revised till you've been down the Forge first thing to check your odds.

First thing, I go down to check my odds for English, down the long side of the building, round the back of technology and there it is, just as I was saying, chock-a-block with people from my year group. Paul's doing good business; I can't get in but I can see through the window. He's like one of those Hindu gods with a dozen arms, his hands are everywhere, taking bets, changing the odds, rummaging in the formbook. He never takes a bet without adjusting the odds slightly, it's like the Stock Exchange, and he never gives odds without thumbing through his formbook. Kids would give a lot for a glimpse of that book, it has the lowdown on everything and everyone, and it's bang up to the minute too, he makes entries all the time, if he had the dates of our periods down there it wouldn't completely surprise me.

Actually, I have seen a book as well-used as Paul's formbook, but only one: our milkman's delivery book, that gets a fair bit of stick, he has to keep a massive great elastic band round it to stop the pages springing up in all directions like a bramble bush.

I try and edge in at the door, the trouble is, no-one's going out; when they've made a bet they hang around in case they miss anything. Even the boffins are there, Claudia, trying to get a price for her French, very quietly. 'FIFTEEN TO ONE ON,' Paul shouts, though she's right by him. A great knowing hoot goes up, making her blush like wildfire. 'That's not fair,' she whispers. 'TAKE IT OR LEAVE IT,' he scans the rest for a more interesting punter. 'Fifty p. then please...' 'FIFTY P? THAT MEANS YOU'LL WIN THREE AND A HALF.' 'Oh dear...' The coins blur in her purse. 'I'd better make it a pound.' 'POUND THE FRENCH GIRL, FIFTEEN TO ONE ON, PAY HER IN EUROS,' he barks to his mate, who's also taking them down. The swarm moves this way and that, but never out of the door. I'm still not properly in when the buzzer goes. I give up and head for form.

Chapter 10

But lunch-time is crazy. It's an unbelievable day at the Forge, everyone's there, first year to sixth form, I should have known. It's the last day of the interviews - the whole place has been crawling with candidates, governors and people from the education authority all morning, and of course Paul's running a book, coining it in by the looks of things, he'll have to invest in a satchel.

But this time I'm determined to get in, I've made up my mind. You usually can if you're trying to place a bet, there's a kind of code - if you've got money in your hand they sort of let you through. If they can move.

Without warning, Brendan, help, catapults out of the door and almost into my arms. 'Kay! How's it going?' I hang on to my books for dear life - me? ME? The first and second years look up wistfully, they think we're lovers - transfer my weight to the other leg - his eyes brilliant with life, deep, so deeply brown and smiling, on me, taking me in - blow a few strands of hair off my forehead, draw from some hidden compartment my most feminine, enigmatic voice, and say, 'Alright.'

'Who've you got your money on?' *He* doesn't have to stop and compose himself that's for sure; in my critically weakened state I sense him edging me out of the main current, and I understand why. Ah, but the first and the second years, the third, the fourth and the fifth, all there, all taking it in.

The excitement's got to him. He's just busting to talk, and I'm the person, he knows all about our mums gossiping and scheming.

'Put your shirt on Dooley,' lowering his voice a bit, I move my head closer, ah god, imagine this was a cinema queue, hug my books tight as if he were between the pages. I could squeeze the breath out of him and keep him like a perfect dried flower, forever.

'They're going for Dooley you know, mum was on the phone. Put your money on Dooley.'

'Dooley?' Even I'm brought down to earth by that piece of atrocious news. 'But he's too old-fashioned isn't he, he can't possibly be...'

'..Trusted to take anyone into the twentieth century let alone the twenty-first, I know, but there's a split apparently, half of them want someone traditional to stamp out all this politics nonsense and get a grip on us, the other half want a younger version of Goldie.'

'So the traditionals have won then? But the other night...'

'No, they haven't. It's loggerheads. Traditional I said, not archaic. They reckon he's not far off retirement, so if they put him in to keep the seat warm it gives them a chance to draw the lines for the main battle over who's going to take us on in the next century. They're looking for someone to really steer the ship - head for new horizons and all that. They're scared to jump in now in case they get stuck with the wrong one.'

I'm stopped dead: I don't know what to say. I mean, I know he's an old softie really, and he made us feel safe in the first-year, but his mind's preserved in amber, historians would queue to make notes on it.

The pigs. They couldn't wait to lay Goldie to rest so they could turn the clock back ten years. How can people think like that? They're only using Dooley to make a point, it's awful. The point being that they want their children working for exams, not getting involved in POLITICS, for one thing. And for another thing, they don't want to be lumbered with any more heads with POP SINGERS for offspring. They want a donkey they can harness, not someone real.

And I just *know* what they really can't forgive her for, is she kept it private. If she could have wheeled Kate Nantucket in from time to time and let them all have a little piece of her they would have been happy. But she wanted her privacy. And now they're making out she must have had something to hide, like maybe Kate Nantucket was a junkie, or maybe she just got rid of her baby, it didn't die naturally, or perhaps she has AIDS. They gob on the most precious things, I hate them, or I would if I knew who they all were. They make out it was shameful that Goldie was Kate Nantucket's mum.

...Ahh, but the first and second years, the third, fourth and fifth - what must they be thinking as they watch us talk so long and earnestly in lowered voices, out of the corners of their eyes?

'...But the other night....' Tut, how careless of me, forgetting to lower my voice. I lower it now, but too late, the kids around us are gobsmacked with envy, not even pretending to look away. I mutter the gist of what I picked up from mum and his mum when they were sticky-beaking about the candidates - especially their reaction to Fido Dido, I reckon I did a fair job there - but he's not convinced.

'Take my word for it,' he says confidently, backing through. 'See you later.'

He won't of course, but talk about serving up your lines on cue. The kids around just melt away in awe and let me through, I'm well inside before I meet any resistance. You can't move for kids putting money on Dooley, word must have got round, he's already odds-on and the seniors are still backing him. It's funny the way the betting goes. The juniors squeeze in the gaps waving their pocket money. 'Twenty p. on the lady please - hey, it's my turn, twenty p. on the lady, she's got nice earrings.' You can hear them yapping to each other in the crush. 'We're betting for Mr. Dooley, he lets you do drawings'; 'So - we've got the one with glasses. You win more.'

But the seniors know the score, they're piling their money on Dooley. One of the sixth formers thrusts a fiver at Paul. His face goes pale, he tries to change the odds before he takes it, but he can't, the punter rams it at him angrily. The mood changes. Paul slams his tin shut, exchanges hurried words with his partner, and shuts his book.

'Right, no more bets, that's it. The books closed.'

A great 'Ahh' goes up, spiced with a few comments, but the kids know he's got himself in deep this time. The muttering dies down. No-one starts the move for the door, though, it's as if they're waiting for the right note to go on. I've still got the two pounds in my hand - might as well, I think, it's now or never.

'Can I just bet on coming top in English,' I say, as quietly as I can, but a long rising 'oooh' ripples out to the edges, they're all laughing - except me, I'm scarlet, so much for my First Lady touch, glamorous confidant and close companion of the Head Boy I don't think. Oh well. 'TEN TO ONE SAYS YOU WON'T DO IT,' hoots Paul, triumphantly. He thought he'd crashed, but now he's back at the wheel.

Everyone's relieved. We need champions. He cele-
brates by giving me long odds, everyone knows it. I
pay up, abashed.

It's the turning point. I mean, finally there's a move
for the door, but it's blocked by an adult face, a new
one. A few of the younger ones gasp, like in junior
assemblies when a bean-bag's gone missing. It's Fido.

He scans the faces and the board. The odds are still
up there. He's taken it all in, you can tell. There's an
almighty hush. It's his move.

'You've got my name wrong.' Calm. Unruffled.
'Seven to two. Hmm, not generous, is it?'

He comes inside. They part like curtains. He's up
by Paul. He takes a hand out of his pocket. There's
fifty p. He offers it.

An almighty silence. Paul can only do one thing.
Without a word he puts out his hand and takes it. The
wave breaks. A long cheer goes up, followed by an
outbreak of almost gentlemanly applause.

'He won't do that if he gets the job,' a voice calls as
it subsides. Fido finds him with his eyes. 'It would
be no fun if I allowed it.' He's straight-faced, but
quite at ease with us.

'What d'you reckon on homework then?'

'What about detentions...'

There follows the most absurd bit of theatre I've
ever seen. The Forge interviews Fido, complete in his
suit. He sits there while they lob in questions from

the windows, the radiators, the corners of the desks, and answers them all. I'll never forget that. I remember the day I sold Vlad the copy of his own essay, that was a bit exceptional (he managed to get 3-1 against winning the appeal, by the way), but the day Fido took on the Forge was a day that ranked with the very best.

Of course we knew he was more relaxed because of being an outsider, but even so.... After, he walks out to this almost old fashioned round of applause, like a county batsman would, not a whoop or a catcall anywhere.

Funny how one unusual thing conjures up another sometimes. In the dining-room afterwards the candidates are sitting at a special table with all the governors and hoipoloi when a first year tries to squeeze past with his tray, trips on a chair-leg and spills the lot. The usual jeer goes up, nothing special, but of course Dooley, being acting Man-in-Charge takes it into his head to do a war-dance. He silences the hall alright, you don't stand and argue with volcanic eruptions, but more to the point, he's silenced his table of bofs, and they take a long time to start talking again. He's made a bit of a prat of himself.

I'm on Paul's table, not by choice, it's just the last place left, and I can see the look of elation on his face. He can't believe it. Dooley's fluffed it, and saved Paul's bacon.

Chapter 11

Well, this is it, I've got to quit from this now for a couple of weeks, where are we now - File/Quit....

*   *   *   *   *   *

Right, well, I'm quitting for Easter now, I've made my bet, we've got our new young head starting after the holidays and I've got two weeks of solid revision BAH! ARF ARF GROOGH to do. So I'll leave you a couple of blank pages to doodle on, have another go at Vlad's essay, but keep it decent, I don't want to be banned like Vlad, there's two pounds riding on this - and I'll see you in a couple of weeks.

The phone went about half-seven that evening by the way, which means the selection panel must have had a right old ding dong. I was in the bath at the time, but mum's high-octave squeal of delight was enough to tell me. Brendan's mum's lot won the day after all, out-flanked the Dooley lobby and got the man they wanted. So it's a fresh face and the beginning of a new chapter in the story of Chadwell Lane High, starting right after the break. Don't go away now. File/Qu.....

PART 3: ADRIENNE

...Bip. Good afternoon. Kay Downes here resuming transmission from one of our outside stations around the city. Today we come to you from Turner's Meadow where we take a look at the devoted work being quietly performed under our very noses by a group of young environmentalists from Chadwell Lane High led by Head Boy and highly edible DISH, Brendan Price.

Brendan, you've been working on this project for some months now, how's it going? Are your patient efforts beginning to show signs of bearing fruit?

BEEEP.

Sorry about that - it's only me trying to be clever. The truth is, operation Save-Our-Meadowland - Stop Humbolts isn't going very well. There are just four of us left now, trudging through the copse once a week with our pens and our little wooden frames. We must look like art thieves who've missed the bus. We're supposed to be charting the vegetation so we can prove it's an area of special environmental interest, trouble is all I've got so far is grass, can tops and dog dirt, which I don't think are all that vital to the balance of nature.

We're a bit bogged down.

The problem is, our new head - Mr. G. Appleby, to give him his full name - is a bit of a disappointment.

He hasn't been much help at all. It's important to have support. For example, we've got this lovely geography chap who takes all the field trips. He comes from a long line of water diviners, no field trip is complete without at least two days of sheeting rain and tents that leak. He's exceptional, they have half a week down the road at Cheddar or somewhere and they come back, eyes glazed with delirium like they've found the source of the Nile. I just can't get over the types of people that inspire others. I mean in the books they're always so clear-eyed and upright - General Kitchener, Your Country Needs You, that sort of thing - but when it comes down to it the one you'll remember the rest of your born days is nearly always some poor bald git in steamed up glasses and a cagoul. I can't get over that.

Anyway, when we started out with this idea we went to ask his advice and he spent three weeks of lunch-hours with us doing a contour model of the area. 'Let's get to know the *terrain* first,' he'd say, up to his elbows in chicken-wire and plaster of paris. It was good. We set it up in the main hall when we'd finished, that's how we got our first recruits. HUMBOLTS SUPERSTORE WANTS TO DESTROY ALL THIS. ARE WE GOING TO LET THEM. Big banner and a petition. They used to flock round. Mind, there's nothing like a relief model to kind of tidy a place up - I mean you're not going to sprinkle it with scaled down pram-frames, busted glass and CONDOMS are you? I'm telling you I'd have died for the place once we got it done. You can't beat a lick of fresh powder paint.

But that's all changed now. Don't get me wrong, I'm not knocking Appleby, not yet anyway. He's quite trendy in some ways. For example the first day he came he had a damn great suggestions box set up in the front lobby. Must have brought it with him I think, actually it doesn't go *too* well with the maidenhair ferns, Picasso and aquaria, sticks out like a ruddy great blue sore thumb to be honest, but I suppose it's the thought that counts. It's just that, before he came most of the Save-Our-Meadowland - Stop Humbolts group was fifth years. They were allowed to join instead of doing P.S.E. See in Goldie's mind a project like that *was* personal and social, so she gave them the choice - endless questionnaires and worksheets with Mr. Cedric (Happy Harry) Harper, B.Ed., in the library, or the community scheme with Brendan. You can imagine, we weren't short of fifth years.

But Harry's obviously sussed the new head's 'listen to the people' approach and told him he'd like the fifth back in one place where he can keep tabs on them. He especially hated the first lesson of each month when he had to put on his khaki mac and gumboots and come out and check how they were getting along.

Even Parminger's been sniffing the breeze. She doesn't type our letters now, they just go on the pile. You can't have an environment lobby without secretarial back-up, it's just not going to happen.

We sit in the wet with our frames and our one finger of Lindy's Kit-Kat, wrapper scuds towards the fence trying tussocks of grass for size. We should fetch it, but if you can't stop Humbolts, why stop a wrapper. I'm missing games for this. The fifth missed P.S.E., fourth miss games if they want, that's why there's so few of us even though it's Brendan, and the Sixth miss general studies - well, miss the classes, they're allowed to count it as their research project. The way things are going we seem to be doing more for Brendan's project than we do for the meadowland, still that's not his fault. Besides, we're not doing much of anything at the moment, just sitting watching the wrapper crucify itself on a bramble.

*   *   *   *   *   *

The first glimpse I catch is her head bobbing up the incline, then her body, then all of her. I thought, she must be an athlete, not a jogger, all puff and towelling, but a proper serious athlete. She had the stride for it, and the physique. Brendan saw her too, my god he saw her. We stopped not talking and looked. She had that long relaxed stride that seems to cover yards at a time, you had to watch. As she came level she turned off the path and loped over the tussocks towards us. I thought she must be coming to ask the way.

She stopped. Tall, black hair tied back, dark dangerous eyes, pouting mouth, slightly breathless, chest rising and falling. Younger than an adult but unbelievably *there*, if you know what I mean. You couldn't look away. God. She was stunning.

Brendan tries to look in command but he's a complete gonner, shot to blazes. I've dreamed of stopping him in his tracks like that every night and every morning for two and a half years. And I don't need to tell you what happens next. I'd give anything. Now look at him, limp as a spare sock.

'Hello. I'm supposed to join you.'

The shimmer of her running vest changing with her breathing. Hell, she must be a sixth former.

With a blurt Brendan holds out his frame. He's in the final stages of autism. The nerve stations are shrieking hormonal 'state of extreme alert' codes down his wires at one another, mostly passing through the groin area en route, but the surface is flat calm. She takes the frame. For a second it catches her perfectly, like an old master hanging in the Tate, then she has it. Flat calm like the sea, like when a submarine's holed itself on the bedrock a hundred fathoms below.

With quiet enthusiasm he leads her off to demonstrate the survey procedure, explaining our aims and our high hopes of influencing the directors of Humbolts to modify their position. Silly boy, fancy forgetting to introduce her to the group. Oh well, too late now, they've chosen their spot, it's in my area I believe, I expect he's forgotten, and now they're crouching down, right down, heads almost together, and he's explaining to her the particular beauty of couch grass.

Well, isn't this just perfect. Here I am on a wet ruddy Wednesday logging the blades of grass in my three-foot square of mud, just in or out of earshot of *them*, depends which way the wind's gusting, while the rest of my year group's in the warm playing ping-pong. They've managed to find the only bit of my section with a cowslip by the sound of it, or something, how interesting for them.

We spend some time combing through our windswept squares in silence, crabstepping from one to the next like ground-feeders working their little territories, while the sheets of graph-paper flap and tear, and our pencils poke holes in the damp spots. Lindy and her friend have remembered their walkmans, the pigs, but is this environmentally sound I ask myself, surely they're missing the calling cries of the curlew and the plover, and the play of the wind among the elms? On the other hand, at least they can listen to their Kate Nantucket tapes while they're getting wet, wet, wet.

Eventually Brendan calls us together in his decisive head boy voice, the one that I thought had got shrunk in the wash since Appleby took over. It's time we had a meeting to decide where we're going next, he announces as we begin the trudge back. 'Macdonald's?' says Lindy hopefully, a bit too loud cause of the walkman. She never gets a joke, and she never says anything she doesn't seriously mean. New teachers take anything up to a couple of years to figure her out. They know she can be relied on to give a straight answer to the most pathetic question, on the other hand she can crack whole classes up without knowing why. They take a big risk when they pick out Lindy.

'No, where we're going next with the project,' he says, playing her dead straight like you have to, he'll be a brilliant teacher, he's got the right instincts. He certainly managed to single out the star pupil, they're almost arm in arm. 'I want to discuss how we're going to organise the next stage.'

Oh, *stage*. We're working in *stages*, progressing from one to the next. Silly me, I thought we were just swanning around in the cold. Women's arms, she's got, must be cold in that vest now, they've gone goose flesh - makes you more aware of a person I always think, goose flesh, makes you notice their body. He's noticed alright, the pig, I bet he can just see himself draping a blanket round her shoulders.

'Adrienne's just been telling me she doesn't think her father's fully behind the project yet - he's going to need a bit of convincing...'

I tramp behind them boggling with disbelief. Eu. Father's not quite fully behind the project, how *tiar*some. Well why doesn't Adrienne just go and take her father for a long walk. Preferably off the end of a cliff. Honestly, the ruddy nerve. I spend years keeping quiet tabs on Brendan, waiting on the sidelines, patiently, for my turn to come round, and in five short minutes the whole thing's gone through the window, down the tubes, and disappeared for ever. She's walking with him now, and there's something sleek in her style, something I know bitterly I'll never have, not if I live to be a hundred. It makes me feel I'm stumbling over the tussocks like a little piglet trying to keep up, though I'm not. It's the egg, the promise of the unborn baby, she's carrying it with her like a gift, it makes her walk differently, boys pick it up in their sixth sense. They turn tribal. Do you know what I'm talking about? Sexuality. It's just *there*, you can tell. Her womanhood, there for the dominant male. The call of the wild.

Oh dammit, I've gone in a puddle, typical. How come some people just exude like that without really doing anything. It's like, if there was another flood, you just know she'd be in the ark. No matter who drowned, she'd have to be saved to preserve the species. To be impregnated. Hell, now I'll have wet tights all afternoon. I wonder if I can dry them on the radiators. Oh shit, I'm such a *girl*.

Chapter 12

It doesn't do to dwell on things. I'm up in Home Ec. watching the tumble dryer go round, Salty's let me put them in with some tea-towels - watching the dryer to take my mind off my legs, which look even fatter and blotchier than before now *she's* arrived - when the door squeaks ajar and a flop of blond hair pokes round. Paul.

Now what does he want up here?

'Fancy that, just the girl I was looking for.'

Hmm. Interesting. He comes over.

'Nice knees. Dimples. Hadn't noticed before.' (Pause) 'You've been with the new girl haven't you? Appleby's daughter. What's she like then?'

My god, of course - father's not fully behind the wretched project - why didn't I realise.

The headmaster's daughter.

'Didn't you realise then? You must be on another planet, the place is buzzing with it. Fancy being stuck with a prat like that for a dad, looking like she does. Talk about short straw. I bet they got them mixed up in the oven thing at birth - incubator - probably some poor sod out there with a half-wit still wondering what the hell went wrong.'

His eyes are like flames under a pot, and they're cooking something up if I'm not mistaken. Adrienne Appleby. God. Still, you can't have everything. The tights stretch tentacles endlessly around teatowels, bit like those carvings on the vases, ancient Greeks chasing each other to infinity.

I suppose I ought to come clean about Mr Appleby, he's not who you may be thinking he is. I had a feeling it might happen all along, I don't know why - yes, you've guessed it, it wasn't Fido who got the job, it was the other one. They were all so geed up trying to stop Mr Dooley, they didn't take enough care. They went for the 'compromise candidate' - i.e., the one who offends no-one. Mr Appleby got the job, the one we hardly noticed when they all came round, with the glasses and suit. The insurance-clerk.

And Adrienne's his daughter.

Paul takes a breath. Here it comes, the sting.

'How's the old English, then? You've got a bit of a project going, haven't you? That's what I've heard.'

English, my eye, I know what this is about, it's about Adrienne Appleby, that's what. Our new sex-goddess. He's up to something. English. I keep shtum. He can squirm.

'Sorry about the other day. In the Forge - showing you up.' Eugh, groogh. They're so obvious sometimes, who do they think they are? And gorgeous. Just look at him with his ice-blue laughing eyes trying to worm his way in. What does he want, a date with her? Never. Not Paul, surely. Anyway. Why me? 'I'll tell you what, what did I say, tens? I'll give you fourteen to one, how about that?'

'FOURTEEN? You cheeky bugger, I'm better than that. Come on, what are you up to....'

He looks away, laughing, wondering how clean he's got to come.

'What a challenge, though. Think about it. They're all busting their flies over her, but she's the bloody head's daughter. It's brilliant. They don't know whether they're coming or going. This'll be the hottest thing of all time. I need you to help me.'

Blimey.

'What do I have to do, chalk the bets up?'

'No, idiot. Keep an eye on old Price. You're on that flipping save the scrubland thing aren't you? They'll be shovelling money on him. Just keep an eye out for me. If he shows any signs of getting-off with her I need to know pronto. It could cost me a packet otherwise.'

Well that just takes the biscuit. He's got me in that pathetic, appealing look. I try looking iron back but I can't. The tights flop to a standstill.

'You've got a bloody cheek.'

He takes them out and finds the inside foot, fancy that, knows what to do.

'Here, while they're warm, give us a leg.'

He runs the warm tights up one leg then the other. Would he go above the knee if I didn't take them? I take them and tell him to look away, but he just looks at my eyes and smiles while I do the rest quickly. Without warning I blush and go to pieces. That's the second time he's done that to me. Only the other time was public. This is private.

Chapter 13

Very bad news. Mr. Dooley has been suspended. I know, I know what I said about him. He *was* sweet, as long as you did exactly what he wanted. He's had one of his turns again, and lashed out at a first year. Honestly, it's just like a carnival at our place, everyone thinks it's so funny. Except me. I was there.

The thing is, we've got a school council now, I mean a pupil council, it's something Appleby's introduced to discuss suggestions for change. Honestly, I'm so sick of being *consulted*. You drop a pencil soon and they'll have a meeting, as if we didn't have enough on our plates. We'll end up like teachers, I can see it: *'Members of the pupil council have kindly volunteered to come in on your behalf for the first two days of their holidays to look into ways of minimising toilet misuse.'* I'm serious. They want to take a close look at mum before they get off on democracy, it's like a spider's web. She has meetings three nights a week on average. They don't do any good. They cancel each other out - either that, or everyone's so exhausted by the end they couldn't care less what gets decided.

Anyway, what's got decided at staff-student level - level, Jesus - at our place is, wait for it, we can take *walkman's* into the exams. I know there's a bit of noise from the traffic when you're in main hall, but just imagine it, a hundred and forty three walkmans plinking away. Now that's a democratic decision for you. They wanted it so they've got it, and now all the poor devils who haven't got one will have to go out and buy them. I mean just imagine not having one now, imagine being in an R.E. exam, for example, without one. Unthinkable. Besides, it'll be that tinny inside the hall you'll need one to keep the noise of the others out. I reckon they'll have to issue them to the invigilators as well, it'll be like two hours of white noise for them otherwise, they'll be chewing the window frames to get out. Perhaps you can order them from the educational supplies place.

I'm sure we could keep the noise out just as effectively if they piped us to sleep with musak. Mind, I'd be chewing window frames then. As a matter of fact the traffic never bothers me, never has, it's the invigilators that get to me, the way they clack the doors coming in and out with their mugs of tea, clump up the rows, breathe horses' breath down your neck as they discreetly glance at what you've put, and whisper. I could throttle them when they whisper. They drool if a kid has a problem, so they can clump over and have a bloody good *whisper* with him for about five minutes, preferably audible to a range of four rows. Or when three of them get together and decide to have a go at the paper, does that get up your nose or what?

Invigilators are the pits, in my opinion. If you got shot of invigilators I seriously reckon most of the interference would disappear. One ought to be enough, and if she wants to go to the toilet she can do what we have to do. Stick a cork in it.

Anyway, where was I? Oh yes, Mr. Dooley. Someone had to do the job of checking over all the tapes, otherwise you could have had kids sat there listening to their own revision notes - so it was given to him, which I think was humiliating and unnecessary. Old people shouldn't be treated like that. You could tell he was at the end of his tether. We were hanging around the Forge where we'd agreed to have our Save-the-Meadowland meeting, and there he was. Using it. He wasn't to know I suppose, wasn't to know it's *the* number one gathering place, if you want pupil power the Forge is the place, never mind coffee and biscuits in the head's room, and there he was the poor devil consigned to the backside of the school with a pair of headphones on.

We're about to drift discreetly away when a first year walks straight up, clatters through the door and says, loud, to get over the music, 'Is this the place where you make the bets?' Can you believe it? They're so dense. What did he think, it was run on the same lines as a tuck shop? Dooley goes purple, he's probably on his thirteenth straight Guns & Roses and he's had enough. Thinks the kid's taking the mick. Before he knows it he's got to his feet, caught him at the door and landed him one. Felled him cold, like a lumberjack. Trouble is, it was only a sapling and he's been done for it. Suspended on full pay pending an enquiry.

Actually, being suspended on full pay sounds a more than reasonable punishment to me. I mean we'd come in every day of the year for half of what a teacher earns, no sweat - if they suspended you as well the place would be a riot. Kids would kill to get that kind of deal. But I suppose it's not the same for Mr. Dooley. For him it must be a rotten deal.

In the meantime the teachers have had their say about the walkmans, and needless to say have squashed the whole thing. I suppose they were trying to show their support for him, but in my opinion it only makes the whole shambles more pointless. Plus, and they may not have been entirely unaware of this when they took their vote, it has swung the mood of the kids very heavily against Appleby. I mean, if you promise absolutely nothing, zilch, that's fine. But if you promise a whole packet then go back on it, you're in bad trouble.

So by the time the coast's clear enough to populate the Forge again and have our meeting, there are a few angry kids to recruit from. Brendan only has to stress that *Appleby's* digging his heels in on the project, rather than it's us dropping off our perches from boredom at the whole wretched thing - which he does, quite effectively - and we get a number of new recruits. And not just any recruits either. Paul, for example, who's not at all pleased that Apple seems to have designs on the Forge now he's discovered it exists, he's joined up. Mind, he's not too pleased with Brendan using it either, he wants to get on with the important job of taking people's money. I wondered about that first year, the one Dooley clobbered, I mean what would he know about fourth year exams anyway. Why would he be betting? I assumed he must have an older brother or sister, I suppose, but I assumed wrong. Of course, I forgot, Paul's running a book on Adrienne: who's going to be the first to get out with the headmaster's daughter, he's had kids swarming to place bets and nowhere to take them, no wonder he's frustrated.

Just to add to the drama of what's supposed to be our quiet meeting, half way through, there she is, in the doorway. She's found the Forge. The talking stops dead. God, talk about an entry.

'Am I late?'

She's there. Adrienne.

*　　　*　　　*　　　*　　　*　　　*

Casually, trying to look like a form teacher, Paul erases the list of boys' names off the board, and the handful of punters who weren't there for the meeting slink away, leaving a dozen or so hard-core ha ha activists. Janey among them with her Olivetti portable and brown envelopes waiting for the order to strike at the heart of commercial greed and self-interest. Vlad, too, though I'm not quite sure why, probably just doesn't like Appleby. He looks pointedly out of the window when she makes her entrance unlike the rest of us. Riveted, I'd say was the word for us.

Brendan, as usual, trying to take control. You'd think he'd be embarrassed having just spent the last ten minutes rubbing her old man's name in the dirt, but he's not Chadwell Lane head boy and chief public speaker for nothing.

'There's still a bit of space,' he says with a regal sweep at the half-empty room. 'I was going to explain how the community project took off in the first place, so the newcomers can get an idea of how things have developed.'

Interesting. Her sitting there while he tells us how very decent Goldie was compared with the current let-down, her dad. I settle myself for a fascinating talk. If Paul was taking bets I'd have a pound he puts his foot right in it.

Adrienne's interested too. She's got legs a quarter of a mile long and she's planted them right in front of him, they're coming out of his eyes. The rest of us are kind of onlookers to the main event. Not Paul, though, he's quietly lobbing a piece of chalk from hand to hand dreaming of the odds, miss wet-shirt universe would have a job knocking him off the tracks, mind - nor Vlad, who's slid from his window seat and wandered round to where Janey is, for a fiddle with the old typewriter keys.

No-one's particularly distracted though. Brendan's talking about the funeral, how Kate Nantucket had been there all along and we hadn't noticed till the very end, when she sang and we cried.

The keys stop tapping, even Vlad must be affected.

'Why don't we...' Adrienne says at last, quietly, we are in the presence of grief here. In fact, there's something I don't really like about her, I realise; not to do with her having had Brendan panting ever since he first slapped eyes on her up at the meadow - it's to do with this room. What's she doing here? It's ours. The Forge, the project. Goldie. They're nothing to do with her. You don't go barging in on things.

'Why doesn't someone, I mean, ask her if she'd support us.... support the project....'

'Wow.....'

'Who? Kate Nantucket?'

'Why didn't we think of that?'

'Who, Kate Nantucket?'

'You've got to be joking, you can't just....'

'Why not? I wouldn't mind. I'd love to meet her, even if she only shut the door on me.'

'She's back in Canada isn't she?'

The buzzer goes and the point gets dropped. We meet Wednesday at the meadow as usual - last survey session before exams.

Exams.

How do we know she's not just keeping an eye on things for her dad. Kate Nantucket - what does she know about Kate Nantucket?

The Forge empties, except for Vlad and Janey, he must have stopped to help her pack her things away. How gallant.

Chapter 14

Up in the meadowland the grass is sweet. After giving the matter long thought I have pulled myself a stem to suck. Nature can spare it. Her sun's warm on our blouses. There are more of us now the newcomers are here, dotted around our little territories. The survey is coming along. We'll piece it all together soon and have a big photo session for the press. Then things'll start to take off.

Brendan is working quietly on his own square. This is when I like him best, when he's concentrating on something small, not puffing himself up to talk to people.

She's not here, don't ask me why, nor's Paul, or Vlad for that matter. Typical, just there for the protest. So we're down to the core, just the ones who care enough to be outdoors doing the work when they could be somewhere else. We're like sheep quietly cropping the field, with each other but on our own, if you see what I mean. The sun has dried the ground now, we can actually put our knees down without muddying them. They've found some coltsfoot. It makes a difference when you've seen something you actually want to save, though I don't suppose it's any big deal to the experts. Also there were bluebells on the way up, and the birds were busy. Ahhh.

A cry goes up, melodical like at a little kids' party when the presents are opened. They've found something, it draws two or three round then the rest. Maybe a small fritillary, they're supposed to be native to the area, hope they've been careful not to bruise its wingtips.

As we crowd round I catch sight of her for the second time, running faster this time, in uniform, directly towards us as if something's wrong.

The ring kind of looks up through Brendan's eyes, he's at the centre now holding what ever it was, brooch I think, they were trying to get the dirt off without damaging it. She bounds the remaining hundred yards or so to where we are. This girl is an athlete alright, school uniform looks about as right on her as one of those little chambermaid's outfits they use in pantos to show off the lead's vital parts. It's not that the buttons are about to ping off, she's not massive chested - it's just something about the way she carries herself, upright and loose-limbed you could say, makes a uniform seem absurd.

What's someone like that missing games for? You can't tell me that makes sense.

'Dad needs to see you....' She flicks away the slip irritably, like a whisp of tobacco smoke, between breaths. 'The head wants you straight away. I think it's quite important.'

Him: 'Any idea what about?'

Us: gawk, drool.

Her: 'Just said to fetch you. Seemed a bit hot under the collar though.'

She should know, she's the one who sits at the breakfast table with him in the mornings, not us. Why is it whenever her and Brendan are in the same vicinity the rest of us feel like teaspoons in a coffee ad. Or maybe it's me. He gives her his frame and jogs off. First team regular he might be, but he can't run like she can. Eventually she looks at me, though no-one said I was in charge, and I show her the bit he was doing.

She needn't think I'm going to be civil though. I turn back to my section, which happens to be quite close, and pointedly ignore her. She's not interested in this. She's been sent to keep an eye on us, that's all. She's spying for her dad.

We carry on like before, well, not quite like before, the cloud's come over. Actually, it's easier to see what you're drawing when the sun's in, but not so warm of course.

'How about a break then?' one of them calls out, new recruit, can't take the blistering pace obviously.

'Hang on, I've nearly done my bit, 'nother five minutes...'

       *   *   *   *   *   *

I wonder what Apple wanted. Something petty, what's the betting. I look over at his first lieutenant without thinking - check she's not recording my thoughts I suppose - and behind the curve of her back catch sight of Brendan coming towards us again. He's not in a hurry, but he doesn't look too happy either. He's kind of stomping.

Standing, crouching, we turn to him. He makes a kind of 'no-good' gesture as he covers the last few yards, like a shop-steward who's been unable to save his lads from redundancy.

'It's finished. The whole project's finished.'

'What?'

'Finito. We're banned.'

People get to their feet, come within earshot without re-forming. Except Janey, talk about dedicated, she's going to finish her square, ban or no ban. Either that or she's out of range.

'Humbolt's chairman's had a death-threat. They're accusing us.'

A dog chases back and forth for whatever his master's throwing.

'Death-threat?'

'That's not fair. How does he know it's us? Anyone can use a phone.'

'It was a letter. Typed.'

'That's what he says. How do we know?'

'What do you think I've just had shoved up my nose for the last ten minutes. There definitely is a letter, and they say we've written it. He wants to see all of us. Now.'

There's a click - Lindy's walkman. Off. This is serious.

'We didn't write no letter. We don't even know where he lives. Least I don't, I'm prepared to swear on oath.'

'He could've done it himself and took it round to Apple to discredit our campaign.'

'Yeah, Apple wouldn't twig - he doesn't even come from round here.'

The dog barks once. The owner throws. Adrienne looks her in the eye.

'Sorry.'

Brendan lobs up a glance.

'What do you mean, discredit our campaign: we haven't got a campaign, we've got about ten of us picking our noses every week on a piece of wasteground, that's not a campaign.'

'It will be when we've done this bit, when we've got the press in.'

Brendan's done in.

'Look, there's no ruddy campaign, right. We're banned. Someone wrote a threatening letter, it wasn't the chairman of Humbolt's. He hasn't been sat up a tree with a pair of binoculars shitting himself for the last three months in case we finish and get an inch in the Chronicle. Someone else wrote it.'

'Charming. That's the thanks we get.'

'You're the one that persuaded us.'

'Yes, well that was before Goldie died. Things are different now. Who wrote the letter?'

We just look at one another in disbelief. It's not the letter - how can you take a thing like that seriously - it's the way he's got everyone's backs up for no reason. This is mister Charm we're talking about now, not just your common or garden sixth former.

'There.'

Janey stands up, she's finished her square. She folds the paper and gathers up her bits.

'What? What's everyone staring at?'

We weren't staring, we just seemed to all look very hard at the same time. It was obvious.

'It was you ...'

She goes fiery red and has a bit of difficulty with the frame. Sometimes you just know when the game's up.

'....I'm *sorry*. There's no need to look at me like that. We were only trying to get things going a bit more.'

'Who's *we?*'

She's got her jaw down like a pelican. Don't give up the agony column just yet Janey, you couldn't lie your way out of a paper bag.

'Don't tell me. Vlad.' It's himself Brendan's angry with, for not spotting it before. 'Shit. You've managed to get things going alright. Apple must be rubbing his hands with glee, he's been wanting to put the mokkas on this ever since he came.'

A blackbird makes that frenzied piping sound they make when they're disturbed. It'll take more than Humbolt's to wipe them out. Brendan's realised what he's said.

'Sorry, Adrienne... Listen....'

She drops her frame and turns away. He's about to go after her. She turns back.

'I have been listening. All I ever hear is Goldie Goldie Goldie. Goldie this, Goldie that. I don't believe it. What was she, Mother Theresa? You're kidding yourselves. No-one's that good.'

He goes to reply, doesn't know how to.

'People aren't interested in your poxy project. They want somewhere decent to shop, they can't park in town.'

She turns away again and makes off, anywhere, just away.

Brendan's wrecked, he's lost more than a project. He rounds on Janey in frustration, till she's in tears and they stop him even though she deserves it.

I leave my things and go after Adrienne. Don't ask me why. Impulse, I think.

Eventually she turns. We're in the copse area.

'Oh... What do *you* want?'

I don't really know, to be honest. I hadn't thought. Her heckles are well and truly up, she's gone blotchy.

'I saw you staring at me. Doing the squares. You were clocking me like I was some kind of enemy of the nation or something.'

'I know. I'm sorry.'

It takes the wind out of her sails. Mine too, I hadn't intended to get feeble.

'It takes a while to adjust, that's all. It's not like she just retired.... we were at the funeral.'

'Adjust. You don't have to tell me about that. I spend my whole life adjusting. Every time he gets a new job I have to bloody adjust. I hate it. You wouldn't know what it's like unless you came from a teacher's family.'

So that was the impulse.

'I do.'

Something goes from her face. The distrust. Her shoulders drop.

'Which one? Does he take us?'

'She. She's at the primary. The green blazers.'

'Ahh. You jammy sod.' She reaches for a branch and takes the weight off one leg. 'I've had to put up with him since I was eleven, he's so awful in school. It wouldn't be so bad if the kids liked him.'

I shrug. There's not much you can say really. She must be really bottled up.

'I dread exams, you know why?'

'Why does anyone?' I try and joke about it.

'I'm always petrified I might come top. He's so big on achievement I'd never live it down.'

A penny drops.

'Is that why you don't do games?'

She nods. 'Won medals where we were before. For the county. You know what he did? He actually rang the local paper and got them to do a feature on us. The Appleby double act or something. Talk about stealing the show. No-one spoke to me for a week.'

This could go on - it must be dreadful for her, but she seems to realise she's had her five pen'orth.

'...I still say you should ask Kate Nantucket. He couldn't do anything if you got her involved.'

She lets go of the branch, ready to go back.

'Where's their house, anyway.....'

'You're practically on the doorstep. It's down there, about half a mile.'

She looks appealingly.

'Just a quick peek?'

I shrug again. 'It's on the way back, if we go round. Hope someone thinks to take my frame.'

We pick our way down till we get there. It's not that big actually, but it's on its own and it's got quite a high fence round. You can't mistake it, there's a massive cedar tree at the bottom growing right out over the footpath. She looks up and down.

'What are you like at climbing? Here, just give me a lift.'

I must be mad.

Cedars have kind of flat circles of foliage getting smaller towards the top. The branches are huge, you feel quite safe once you're up there. I've never seen the back of Goldie's place before. It's got french windows and an uneven patio. He's in there talking to someone, there are great hulking settees, looks like the fleet's in dock.

We sit for a while, getting used to it. He crosses in front of the windows, Mr. Threadgold, I recognise him, then comes back. He's got a book or something, looks as if he's got it to show someone else, I can't see, they're not in view.

I want to get back down. I feel like a spy, I didn't think you'd be able to see in like that. It doesn't look as easy as it did coming up.

Whilst I'm trying to figure it out, a catch is unlocked sharply and with a sigh the french windows open. His voice comes through first, you can just hear it. He must be showing his visitor something. We freeze, though we're quite well-concealed and not that close. Just as long as our blouses don't stand out too much. What on earth am I doing up a ruddy tree in the first place? Fortunately they're looking down at something, shrubs I think, or some small flower, she's come out with him, a woman of about mum's age, perhaps a bit younger. Adrienne's craning her neck like a hawk but it's not her, not Kate Nantucket. I can tell that straight away.

A chap comes to the french windows. He doesn't join them, just stands there taking in the sun on the garden. He runs his eye over it in a casual sort of way, just taking in the feel of the season rather than anything in particular. He settles on the tree where we are. Hell's bells. He hasn't seen us, he's looking at the top, but I've seen him, and I know who he is. It's Fido. The chap with the socks.

I grip tighter on my branch. What's he doing here? What's he doing anywhere round here, come to that, surely if you don't get a job you just go back wherever it was you came from don't you? He wasn't from here he was Yorkshire I think, somewhere like that. Yes, Riding. I thought he must be a horseman when mum first said it.

God. If Adrienne knew.

Something's certainly got him about the tree, he's impressed, he's bringing his eye slowly down from the top, taking in the grandness of it or something, he's not going to look away till he's reached the bottom, that's for sure, and I'm not too certain our blouses can't be seen if you're looking straight at them. I've developed a desperate itch.

As if at a signal all three of them look to the house. Must be a caller, I can't hear a phone. Mr. Threadgold goes in and leaves the other two.

We breathe out in unison. They're not concerned with the garden now, they're talking. Mr. Threadgold's back, he's opening a letter. The person who's brought it must be with him, by the way he's half-turned back towards the room. He reads it while Fido and his lady watch. Yes, he's talking to the caller now, introducing him to the other two.

Heck, I don't believe it. Oh my life. It's Vlad. Vlad goes in where angels fear to tread. He's gained entry.

The door shuts at last, and we're up in our branches jabbering like a pair of gibbons.

'You know what *I* think?'

'Yes. Just like you said. He's gone to ask if she'll take part in the protest.'

'And, what's more, he's been invited in.'

You'd think we were standing outside Tesco's the way we're going on, instead of half-way up a cedar tree. It's such a first-rate, fresh piece of gossip I don't give too much thought to what Fido's doing there, that can wait till I've got time to digest it properly. Don't give too much thought to the chap underneath, either, till he shouts up at us. We look down. He keeps shouting from his reddened, upturned face. Funny, but from up here he looks more ridiculous than we do.

Oh dear. Life gets complicated -

'Please don't get cross Mr. Dooley, we're coming down. We were only looking.'

- specially when you're poking your bare legs round for footholds while someone's underneath watching.

We get to the ground, feeling like four year-olds. He's all flustered, which makes him even more pompous.

'I suppose you've got a suitable explanation.'

'Mr. Dooley, please....'

'As I thought. We'll see what Mr. Appleby has to say about this, shall we? Lucky I was passing, perhaps I might mend a few fences with him. Come on - both of you.'

Oh dear.

'Mr. Dooley....' This is how he must pass his time now, walking the footpaths chewing things over and over, I could cry for him.

'I suppose your friend's got a name? Well? Has she?'

Without a single word Adrienne starts, and with a parting, imploring glance at me bounds through the bracken like a gazelle and is gone. His face shatters into fragments. They run from him like dogs from a vagrant. In desperation he lunges for the world he's losing and claws for a grip.

'Mr. Dooley you're hurting. Please let go....'

But he marches me stinging with anger and humiliation all the way. I'm not crying by the time we get there, but I'm in tears - not because they stopped what they were doing and stared at us out of the classroom windows, and not from the pain of his clamping, bony grip, but because of the time he used to let me collect and give out in the first year; how he's reduced to using me now to impress someone who's moved into the place that was his, and pushed him out. Someone no older than his son might be. I see his desperation close up and it's ugly and pitiable.

It's no good, I'll have to have a blub.

Apple isn't in his office when we get in, or when he gets me in, I suppose I should say - Mrs. Parminger kind of has to prize me gently from his fingers and thank him like you do a labrador that's fetched the paper. When he's gone, back down the long drive to resume his suspension, she rubs the circulation back for me, and I know from her manner that he's brutalised me for nothing, nothing at all. She probably won't even bother to mention it to anyone.

Chapter 15

Thank God for exams. Who says they're no fun? Another day like that and I reckon a game of 'he' with a pack of starving wolves'll seem like fun.

Anyway, there's no permanent damage, except we are definitely banned, it's official. The meadowland project's over and Humbolt's rules. Ah well, games isn't so bad.

I'm actually quite excited getting ready, I mean I've done as much revision as I can, so you never know I might do alright. I'm nervous and neat, like a new pupil. Mum's all done up too, she's having her photo taken with her class. She gives me a kiss and a hug, leaving lipstick on me.

The place is buzzing when I get in. We may not have walkmans but we've got mascots of every shape, size, colour and description, some of them take up that much room you might as well give them a candidate number and stick them in for the exam themselves; we've got polo-mints, gum, dried flowers; we've got a desk covered in birthday cards; and best of all, we've got sun. When you see those panels of sunlight warming the wood in a great hall full of desks you know it's going to be alright.

Adrienne comes over for a natter, we get on alright now, since the showdown among the cedars. She still turns heads all over the hall, can you believe it THIS GIRL IS A FOURTH YEAR, any younger and she'd be a freak - as it is she's just stunningly well-developed and attractive. Oh well, as long as she keeps talking I might get noticed too.

The invigilator calls us to order and gives instructions. Vlad walks in right on the start time, aloof and disdainful, he always goes like that when he's in trouble - the exact opposite of everyone else. He's been suspended for the letter to Humbolt's: they're letting him sit the exams, then he's out for a week. Actually some of the wags are already calling Appleby 'Absentee', because of the suspensions, but I suppose he had to do something.

I'm completely immersed in my paper, science, multiple choice, what a breeze - as a matter of fact I've often wondered whether the order of answers is random, or if Mr. Purnell sits there thinking, 'We'll have another D there, they won't be expecting that, then I'll do three A's and an E...' Anyway, I'm plodding through quite happily when I become aware of this spasmodic tapping sound. Paul's noticed it too. He's a couple of rows over from me, but he's all ears and eyes like a feral cat.

It's Adrienne. She's brought a dice in her pencil-case and she's rolling it whenever she doesn't know an answer. I'll be damned. That's a hell of a way to do multiple choice. I actually watch Paul for several minutes, I love it when you get chains like that - someone watching someone watching someone -, and he is absolutely nailed down with awe. Fixated. He's found a kindred spirit. He just can't wait to get across to her afterwards and check that little knuckle-bone for himself. He's priceless, honestly. There are about a hundred and ten boys in that hall who'd give their teeth to run the thumb over *her*, but it takes a dice to bring out the curiosity in Paul, he can't bear the thought of someone else rolling lucky numbers with it, not him. He's got to be there. He's jealous.

He spends the clearing-up time throwing sixes for her and then - pif paf poof - out come the cards and he's there showing off till the dinner-ladies turf them out so they can set for lunch.

By mid-week she's got her confidence though, and the dice has gone: she's beginning to bid for run-on sheets. Vlad, on the other hand, has absented himself, decided to punish them with their own weapon I suppose and refrained from putting in any further appearances. In a state of tingling excitement I take up my pen for the English, write absolutely nothing for five minutes paralysed by the thought that he might make a dazzling late entrance, and then rip my way through sheet after sheet in such a closed-off trance that the 'five minutes' call hits me in the ribs like a dum-dum. I stack my thirteen curled sheets lovingly together and hand them in. I have fulfilled my mission WOOP WOOP WOOP. DIVE AND HEAD FOR HOME.

But Vlad has been frying bigger fish, I should have known. Trust him to trump me without even writing a line. He's got Kate Nantucket to do a concert, the first since Goldie's death, in support of the project. He's all over the Chronicle and on the regional news. The following Monday when he's supposed to start his suspension, he sweeps up to the main doors in a TAXI, the poser - quarter to ten - and within the hour he's back in and Save-Our-Meadowland is back on in a big way. We've got a two-page spread in the next issue if we can pull our fingers out and finish the survey.

Now that's class.

*   *   *   *   *   *

But that's not the only thing. It's happened. Brendan and Adrienne. I could kick myself. The school's full of it. I was so wrapped up in the exams I just sat there and let it happen under my nose. And

I mean right under my nose - it was the day Mr. Dooley caught us up in the tree.

What with all the excitement about the concert and the project being back on we had another meeting in the Forge. It didn't quite go to plan though, not that there was a plan, because Brendan was late, which is unusual for him. In the meantime Vlad made the most of his overnight stardom and took us through how he'd buttered up Mr. Threadgold, that must have been when we were watching from the tree, though I didn't say, it wouldn't have been fair to steal the limelight - besides Adrienne wasn't there to back me up. Vlad strings it out a bit, how at the very time we were scratching our pens uselessly along hundreds of sheets of file paper in the hall he was back at the Threadgolds drinking coffee with Kate Nantucket herself and negotiating the concert - when in they come. Him and Her. Together. There in the clear light of day. She sits quite near him as he unfolds all the finished survey sheets and explains how they're going to be put together for the display. Obviously they've got it all squared with our geography man to tidy things up and mount it properly - we've just got to get it finished off as soon as we can.

And out they go, together. Vlad, finding no call for more fascinating details of his initiatives on the community's behalf, leaves as well, and then the real meeting starts. Rumour has it that while Dooley was dragging me in one direction for a showdown with Mr. Appleby, Brendan had slipped off in the other direction for a showdown of his own with the apple of Appleby's eye: Adrienne. The lousy pig, he followed us - it was one of those chains, him watching us watching Mr. Threadgold - and when Dooley came along, instead of riding through the forest to my rescue, he let him drag me off and went after Adrienne. And I don't have to tell you what kind of showdown it was either. Rumour has it you couldn't slip a *feeler*-gauge between them by the time they'd finished. I could die of misery, I mean it.

I shouldn't think Paul's overly pleased with the turn of events either, he must owe a fortune. So he didn't get his early warning off me after all, serves him right, and to think, I was there all the time. There's one thing I could give him an early warning about, though - quite a few people are after him for their winnings. But I imagine he must know already. He's keeping a very low profile at the moment, is Paul.

Chapter 16

I'm having a damn good lie-in after all my exertions of the last week or so, vaguely aware of mum and Mrs. Price downstairs hard at the Saturday morning natter, honestly, they're like a pair of hedgerow birds those two - I won't say I'm not fantasising - Adrienne has a terrible fall on a rock-climbing trip, I risk several life-or-death situations to get help; it's only when we're both visiting her bedside that Brendan realises he loves me not her; he has a student flat (he's at Uni now) round the corner, I try to resist for her sake but his lips are soft and his arms so strong.... that sort of thing - when the door rattles and wangs itself open and a weight settles itself on my bed. No, not Brendan, but the nearest thing to him I suppose. Not that it helps. Trishia, his sister. She could have given it another five minutes, just till I'd got past Adrienne's funeral and, alone at last, fallen tear-stained with grief into his arms, but not to worry, there'll be other times.

'Mum wants to know if you can baby-sit me tonight before she goes... Can you then?'

I sit up with a grunt and rub my eyes. She's there alright, gleaming with sunlight and zing.

Groogh.

'Well?'

'When? Tonight, or before she goes?'

'Eh?'

'Doesn't matter. Just say yes. What time?'

'D'know. I'll shout it up.'

She nips to the door.

'What's wrong with Brendan, anyway?'

She does a plie.

'Girlitis.'

'Who? Who this time?'

Might as well just confirm the facts, since she's here. But she knows. Sixth sense. She darts behind the door.

'Tell me.'

'TRISH, WHAT ARE YOU DOING?'

Mrs. Price. Thinks she's playing me up. She is.

'IT'S ALRIGHT MRS. P.... ABOUT WHAT TIME?'

'EIGHTISH...? AND DON'T FEEL YOU'VE GOT TO PUT UP WITH ANY OF HER NONSENSE. TRISH, COME DOWN NOW.'

She swings back round and puts her tongue out:

'Don't put up with any nonsense now...'

'Trish, who? She's called Adrienne, isn't she?'

'Don't know, I've only heard them on the phone. Someone he does that grassland thing with.'

'TRISH. NOW.'

'The meadowland project?'

She nods and bobs off. Damn. It must be serious then.

The front door finally goes. The wall stares. Not much point going back to the funeral now, we'll have to postpone it, she can die another time.

Mum comes up with a coffee. Instead of dumping it on the dresser and flinging the curtains open, she carefully sits herself on the bed beside me. Blimey, she must be troubled about something.

'Are you alright Kay? Shall I leave you a bit longer?'

I blink. Me?

'You mustn't feel....' she says, all tentative and churned up. 'You mustn't feel you can't talk to us about anything. You mustn't feel you couldn't bring someone back here to meet us. You wouldn't feel like that, would you....'

Help, I can't take group therapy this early. I have a long sip and look through the steam at her. What have they been going on about down there?

'What's up mum?'

She finds a mark in the duvet.

'Nothing... Gloria was just saying - I suppose it doesn't matter - that Brendan's been chopping and changing his girlfriends lately, and she feels, well, in the *dark* I suppose...'

Hmmm. She should be so lucky. I wish I was in the ruddy dark about Brendan's girlfriends.

There's more.

'At last nights' governors' meeting Gloria says she was talking to Mr. Appleby over a glass of red wine and he let it slip that he has exactly the same problem. He's sure his daughter's found herself a boyfriend in the school but when they try and bring the conversation round to it she storms off. It must be very difficult for him, I mean in his position....'

'Why?'

I look over the cup. The steam's gone, and her train of thought's as clear as a bell. Bloody nerve, fancy trying to wheedle a thing like that out of me.

'Well, I.... he wouldn't want to be made a laughing-stock or anything, would he? You can't blame him for that.'

'Tell him to get a new suit then.'

I'm out of bed and heading for the bathroom. Briskness is the only thing at a time like this. Ha, both of them, Apple and Mrs. P., what a giggle, both completely in the dark, unlike the rest of the entire school. If only they knew. Actually I'd tell the man in the moon if it meant him seeing five minutes less of her, I would honestly. But not them. They can find out for themselves.

I hope the water's warm.

Chapter 17

Paul has finally been run to ground and forced to pay up. I think some of the rugby team gave him a bit of encouragement - anyway, he's arranged to dole out first-to-date-Adrienne winnings at the Forge, lunchtime. There's a big crowd, and a big crowd atmosphere, at the appointed time, but no Paul. A lot of banter about the Securicor van being held-up, that sort of thing. It's another balmy spring day and half the sixth form are preparing to line their pockets with Paul's life savings. But Paul's savings haven't turned up, and nor has Paul. The padlock's still on the door. The blinds are down.

'He's probably in there swinging from the light-flex,' someone calls out. There's a lot of laughter, but no more jokes. We become tense. He owes quite a lot of money. By the time they prize open the window the atmosphere's frightening.

But he's not there thank God. Something is though. The rest of the blinds go up and the windows are flung open onto a scrawled message on the easel. 'BETTER LUCK NEXT TIME SUCKERS'. There's a photo-booth snap pinned to the top. Paul and Adrienne. Kissing. However many times they rip it up and stamp on it, it's them.

Which makes for an interesting little conundrum: if Adrienne really is going with Paul, and he hasn't just put her up to it, which I can't believe Brendan would allow - besides, that would mean she's actually going with Brendan after all, like everyone says.... But if she really has got herself off with Paul - then who the devil's Brendan going with?

That little tease Trishia. I wish I'd have known about this on Saturday, I'd have wrung her neck.

*　　*　　*　　*　　*　　*

ADRIENNE. WHAT ARE YOU READING? R.S.V.P.

Bowering's completely immersed at his desk, marking exam papers. You could pass tablets of stone never mind notes, he still wouldn't know. Not unless you dropped them.

JANE EYRE. STARTED AT THE OLD SCHOOL.

CRICKEY BIT HEAVY ISN'T IT? JUST LOOK AT BOWERING. I LOVE THE WAY THEY MAKE YOU WORK LIKE STINK IN YOUR OWN TIME BUT THINK ITS PERFECTLY OK TO TAKE A WEEK OFF TIMETABLE WHENEVER THEY'VE GOT A BIT OF WORK TO DO, DON'T YOU?

Bowering does, anyway, he's not even subtle about it, just tells us to bring readers for the week and keep out of his hair.

P.S. DONT YOU LIKE JUDY BLUME THEN?

READ THEM ALL IN 2ND YEAR

O LA DI DA NO NEED TO RUB IT IN. IS IT TRUE YOURE GOING WITH PAUL BY THE WAY SOME OF THEM ARE SAYING THE PHOTO IS A FAKE

WHAT PHOTO?

God. Good job she's sitting over the other side.

NOTHING, JUST TEASING. SO YOU ARE ON WITH HIM THEN?

WHAT PHOTO?

Oh dear. She looked like that when she came within an inch of tearing me limb from limb up at the copse.

WILL YOU ANSWER MY QUESTION IF I ANSWER YOURS?

I AM GOING WITH HIM YES. HE'S CUTE

HE'S CRAZY YOU MEAN. WHAT ABOUT BRENDAN, I THOUGHT YOU WERE GOING WITH HIM. ITS ALL ROUND THE SCHOOL. ARE YOU....(TWO TIMING)? NAUGHTY.

Luckily she's beaming all over her face, it could have easily gone either way.

YOU MUST BE JOKING, BRENDAN? HE DID ASK ME BUT I TOLD HIM TO STICK TO POLITICS. NOW, KAY, WHAT PHOTO?

Correction, it has gone either way.

I'M SORRY I THOUGHT YOU KNEW. THERE WAS A PICTURE OF YOU AND PAUL PINED UP IN THE FORGE AT LUNCH-TIME.

- OF ME AND PAUL WHAT?

KXXXING

She goes fiery red.

THE DIRTY LITTLE SKUNK. WAS HE RUNNING A BOOK ON ME?

I DON'T THINK SO

YOU LIAR. WAS HE??

I nod, pathetically. She sweeps a forefinger across her throat and grimaces. I *think* she means Paul. I hope she does.

The door opens and Janey walks in, late from her stint in the library. Did I say walks, god just look at her, she's got a touch of make-up - first time I've ever seen her with it - her hair's swept back; she's got six inches taller and filled out in the right places all in the space of one winter, and none of us noticed.

She sits down and takes her book out.

..... oh yes they have. *Some*one's noticed alright. Brendan. Don't ask me why, I just know it. I could kick myself - what a fool.

DEAR JANEY,

MY PROBLEM IS I HAVE A FRIEND WHO IS RATHER KEEN ON THE <u>HEAD</u> <u>BOY</u> AT OUR SCHOOL BUT SHE IS PETRIFIED TO APPROACH HIM IN CASE HE SAYS NO. WHAT SHOULD SHE DO? A WELL-WISHER

Her smile is like a locket, it holds a picture.

DEAR WELL-WISHER,

THIS PROBLEM HAS NOW BEEN DEALT WITH QUITE SATISFACTORY THANK YOU FOR YOUR CONCERN.

Ah.

Ah-so.

No, I can't mimic my way out of this one. I always thought there was a chance of developing into something special overnight, it's just that Janey never even crossed my mind when I thought it. Oh no, she can't be, please....

A voice from Bowering's desk: 'May I see the notes, Kay. They look fairly advanced now.'

Not even looking up from his papers, how cool can you get. The rotten pig.

'Please.... Hmm.'

He has a good old butcher's *hook* while the class waits in glee -

'I wouldn't say Jane Eyre was that bad.'

- and hands them courteously back.

*   *   *   *   *   *

Did I say Vlad's got class? Well, he's not the only one. You don't expand during a recession unless you're a bailiff, or you've got a bit of class yourself. We get the two-page spread alright, but we've been scooped for the headlines:

DEATH-THREAT LETTER: HUMBOLTS BRING IN POLICE.

Front page. There's a picture of Mr. David Humbolt holding it up to the light, god knows what for but it looks impressive, and at the bottom of the page is a mug-shot of our tight-lipped Mr. Gordon

Appleby, M.Sc., P.G.C.E., with the caption 'Head Remains Silent'. Can't think why, even the paper must know it was Vlad, except they can't actually name him, he's still a juvenile. 'Seeking legal advice,' it says - Apple obviously trying to protect the school's reputation, to hell with Vlad, he can protect himself. Typical.

They do a fair bit of advertising in the Chronicle, do Humbolt's.

Chapter 18

I'm trying to make myself get out of bed. I don't think I've ever felt this low about school before - it's just an endless way of killing time and rotting your brain. Day after day after day. I've had off days, like everyone else, but I don't think I've ever had it as bad as this. I feel like I'm never going to see the end of it.

The concert's off of course - her agent got on to the school the second the news hit her doormat - and so is the project: the whole display's been ripped down and trashed, all our work. There was no need for that, it was vindictive, which sums Appleby up in my opinion, I always said he would blow with the wind, right from the day he came round as a candidate. Like a crisp bag.

Vlad's been re-suspended, they practically frog-marched him off the premises. I know it's his own fault, you can't go round threatening to kill people even if they are poisoning the planet; mind, he wouldn't know how to *draw* a gun, let alone get hold of one and set it off. Honestly, the whole stupid lot's just a play-act, no-one does anything real. He was the only one, Vlad. He might have been a pain, but at least he had the guts to go up to people and put them on a spot. All we did was get mud on graph-paper. It wasn't real at all, it was just killing time. Come to think of it I'm glad it's gone in the bin. It's where it belongs. Humbolt doesn't need showing how many species of grass there are, he knows. He deserves to be threatened.

To cap it all we can't even be told our exam results. They're going to make a little *game* of it. Because we don't all get the privilege of joining our mums and dads in the annual roll-over in their children's achievements on prize-giving night - on account of the lack of space - the school pupil-teacher council has come up with the wizard wheeze of having *two* prize-giving ceremonies, one at the end of half-term in school, to give us the chance to revel in glory and humiliate the losers, and then the regular orgy for parents in the last week before the holidays, as usual.

In the meantime we can all have this lovely communal *thrill*, daydreaming our way through the next fortnight's lessons wondering how well or badly we've done, flirting with our favourite teachers while they sprinkle the ground with little hints for us to fight over, and cake themselves in their sudden gush of popularity.

I haven't really introduced you to my dad have I? That's because we don't get on too well, he has a foul temper which he's always taken out on me rather than mum - plus he has an even more embarrassing job than her, Education Welfare & Attendance Officer. He has to persuade the school phobics to go back and give it another try. We spend a fortune sending in home tutors and the rest, gradually weaning them back, and then a teacher goes and shouts at their class and the whole process goes right back where it started. Funny thing though, they don't start out as galloping school phobics - something must just push them over the edge and made them realise what a useless lot of nonsense it really is I reckon, and after that they can't bring themselves to go near it again.

I feel like that. I feel if I go through those gates once more I'll get radiation sickness and my hair'll start dropping out. School might appear safe, but it's colourless, odourless, and it's deadly.

I grope downstairs. Mum's had her Vitalite and cottage cheese I see. Pile of exercise books on the side, you can't even get away from it in the sanctity of your own home, they'll have school report wallpaper next. Letters - one from gran, can't be bothered now, it'll only be about her latest visit to the specialist. Poor old gran, when you're a kid it's teachers that poke and probe into every nook and cranny of your life, when you're old it's doctors. What else? Ooh, she's had her school photos, must have been looking at them over the toast. Just look at her, talk about mother hen and her chicks. The one on the end looks a right saddo. The other pic's a staff shot, mum all prim and proper, knees together like in all the other years. Honestly, when I leave I reckon I'm going to be a school photographer, and I'm going to specialise in *real* poses, kids smoking up the delivery bay, that kind of thing, standing in the corridor when they've been turfed out of class, snogging in the corners at disco's. Mr. Simms' lot playing five-card brag in the staffroom in their lunch-hours, and arguing about the best looking sixth-formers. We know. I'll make a fortune.

Mum's pictures just confirm what a life-sentence the whole thing really is, they go back years, we've got an album of them, all they do is show folk getting older, losing hair, gaining worry lines, wearing duller clothes, and disappearing. They actually seem to sit in the same positions every time, so I suppose if you took the whole collection and flicked through it like a pack of cards you'd see the process speeded up. Makes you shiver.

On such joyful thoughts and a bowl of shreddies I prepare to leave when my eye catches something I hadn't noticed. The lady in Mrs. Russell's place - the one who retired last summer, they bought her a hanging basket, ugh, groogh - I recognise her.

Can't think where, though.

'Mum... Who's this?'

She comes in flapping for her keys.

'Not now Kay, can't you see?...' Looking under the cereal packets - desperate, my mum, mustn't be late think of all that learning they'll miss - 'Where? Oh her, Mrs. Olney, you don't know her. Just down from Yorkshire. Ahh...'

They're under the other picture, silly me. Mum scoops the lot up, including what I'm holding, and leaves the room.

'Wait, mum....'

Yorkshire, yes. Olney. It's Fido's wife, I saw her up the cedar tree. I mean -

'But what are they doing down here? Surely -'

'What do you mean, "what are they doing?" This isn't Iraq. Will you get ready, I'm not having you strolling the streets like a latch-key kid with her parents off at work. Why shouldn't they come down here if they want. And don't forget the table. Now, bag, keys, books.... Honestly, I think there's a new mood of intolerance. Handbag.'

'But he didn't get the job, did he?'

'Who didn't? Kay, you're going to be late.'

'Mr. Olney. She's Mr. Olney's wife isn't she?'

'Yes dear, I imagine she is. But not the Mr. Olney you're thinking of. Your Mr. Olney was a teacher unless I'm very much mistaken who came down for an interview and went back again, and her Mr. Olney's a writer. Now I'm going to school, where the children learn to read and write, and grow up, and so are you. And I'll be very cross if the breakfast things are still on the table when I get home. Now, I don't want you to worry about Mr. Olney any more. Mr. Olney's in his heaven and all's right with the world, so WILL YOU PLEASE GET READY. I'll see you later, don't forget your key, I may be a bit late.'

Learn to grow up. Ha. And the rest. Utter garbage. I sweep the things into the sink and wend my way towards the door. What's this writer lark, I wonder. Baffles me.

PART 4: FIDO

Chapter 19

Looks like I'm not the only school-phobic today. I'm wandering aimlessly around at lunch when who should I see just sitting on his own in the Forge, but Paul. No bets today, blimey, things must be flat. Looks like he's got a right one on him, I should have thought he'd be in full swing after the way he stung the punters recently. I go and join him. We can both be miserable together.

'No Adrienne?'

He scowls blackly at me.

'Don't pretend you don't know.'

'Dumped you has she? Serves you right.'

'*That's* not the problem, I'm not bothered about that.'

'What then?'

'Don't you know? No, you missed assembly didn't you. What's up with you...? Anyway, she's dobbed me to her old man about the book-making business. He's had me in already. Says if he had any proof I'd be out. Wish I was, I'm sick of this place.'

God, she doesn't take prisoners then. I sit there looking glum. Book-making business - makes it sound like the Young Enterprise scheme. Still, it did liven the place up. She shouldn't have grassed.

He looks at me. I colour again, dammit, even in this mood. I came in looking for a kindred spirit, and suddenly it's boy/girl. I've got palpitations. He is actually very masculine when he's upset, you could easily mistake him for eighteen.

'Anyway, what's up with you? Not in the library?'

Alright, I know.

'Just fed-up. It's not the same since Apple came. You get committees, but....'

'Ha!' He shifts, as if a sudden gust got him. 'You know what's happened to Vlad don't you? Humbolt's pressing charges. He's got to go to court.'

'How petty. Maybe we should all write him a death-threat, he can't take us all to court. I suppose Apple won't help him...?'

I'm remembering Goldie and the essay. But that was a lifetime ago.

'He'll help put him inside if he can, the prick. You're trespassing in here by the way.'

'Pardon?'

'It's out of bounds. They're turning it into the school shop - scarves, ties, the lot. Just tell me what that's got to do with our education...'

Bit rich, coming from him. I smile.

'You did alright out of it.'

We kind of super-nova into the fresh air. I remember mum's photo.

'Hey, I didn't tell you. Olney lives round here somewhere - Fido Dido. Remember that interview, the time he wandered in?'

'Bet on himself, didn't he. Bad policy. Shouldn't let your heart rule your head.'

Trust Paul to remember the bet. I think about my two pounds.

'We'll see about that. He's supposed to be a writer though, that's what I can't understand.'

There's a spectacular stumping on the field. The pile of jackets has been scattered for yards. You know summer's on the way when first-years start quarrelling over run-outs, they're coming over from the outfield now to get their oar in, it's a proper scrap.

That's involvement for you.

'Listen...' Oh dear, this is new ground coming up. 'Let's find out where he lives and go and call on him. He knows the Threadgolds doesn't he? Maybe he can help.'

He looks me over and shrugs. Can't make me out. Nor can I, come to that. 'Not still bothered about that ecology bollocks are you?'

'Cheek. You joined. I just feel like doing something, you get piles sitting in lessons. Come on, Meadowland Adventure, Nancy Drew and the Hardy Boys. Shall we?'

He shrugs again. He's not that interested in risk unless it's got a price on it.

I get up and lead the way.

'Not the gate, you fool. The fence.'

Talk about green. Down the side of the tennis court and through the gap. Freedom. It's there all the time, just waiting to embrace you.

We cram into a phone-box. We have a situation of extreme closeness here. No good going weak at the knees though, there isn't room. Besides, I'm too scared. I get the number from directory.

'Mr. Olney? The one who applied for the headship at Chadwell Lane High? We wondered if we could possibly come over and ask you some questions. It's for the magazine.' Paul rolls his eyes like an epileptic. 'Er, thank-you, that's very kind. Friday might be too late though, it has to be printed before then. We could make it this afternoon if it's not inconvenient. It wouldn't take long... Oh, thank-you. I'll jot the address down.'

'*Magazine?*' We spill into the street. 'You're not up to this. You wag an afternoon then act like you're still in school, that's daft. You get all the risk and none of the fun.'

'I couldn't think of anything. It would have been suspicious otherwise. Come on - Hardy Boys. You said.'

'Sod the Hardy Boys, let's hit the arcade.'

'No, come on....'

Chapter 20

He comes to the door in builders' dungarees.

'Ah, the one who took the bets. Bad move betting on yourself, I should have known. Come in, watch your feet.'

'God, what a massive place.'

'Don't I know it. Here – there are stools in the kitchen.'

Every room has paint, tools, plaster, bare wires. The breakfast bar has a coating of dust. He sweeps it away with a rag so we can put our elbows down, and plugs the kettle in. There are some mugs in the sink, and in a tea-chest, with newspaper still round. He smiles.

'We eat out a lot. Tea or coffee?'

'I'm sorry, really, we didn't know you were this busy. We'll come back if you like.'

'You'll have a long wait if you do. It'll take years to get on top of this lot.'

'Why did you buy it?'

'Inherited. Wife's mother died a couple of months ago.'

'Oh... sorry.'

'Not to worry. Sugar?'

'Have you given up your job, then?'

He contemplates his tea for a bit. You'd have a job to imagine anyone less like a headmaster, he's got dust in his hair and scabs on his hands from the work.

'Well, we decided I'd put in for your headship, because it was so perfect for the house, and if it didn't come off I'd leave anyway. There are a couple of projects I want to take a shot at. Gives you a few options when someone leaves you a house.'

'Writing projects, do you mean?'

He's startled.

'Mum works with your wife. She's pretty. Don't mention about us coming though, will you?'

He raises an eyebrow.

'No magazine....? Ah, so we're all taking a little time off school, then. Hmm. And you thought you'd come and welcome me to the district, very nice of you.'

'Sort of. Mr. Olney, have you known the Threadgolds for very long?'

He frowns.

'It was you in the tree, then. You get about don't you? No, it was just a coincidence really. I've been meaning to branch out a bit, there isn't a living to be made in fiction. Then when the house came up, and I read about the funeral of your headmistress, I thought I might take the opportunity to approach them once we got settled, if that doesn't sound too callous. What were you after, autographs?'

The tree. I'm scarlet, but it'll have to wait.

'You're writing a book about Mrs. Threadgold?'

'Well, indirectly. Kate Nantucket. Biography. When I'm not planing the bottoms of doors.'

'Wow... Are you famous then? How many books have you written?'

'No; and not enough. But one keeps going. *Was* it autographs, is that what you want me to get you?'

I fan my face. He's making me feel such a fraud. It's time I explained.

'I'm sorry. The tree was just a sort of dare, it didn't mean anything. We didn't come round to ask you to get autographs, honestly. It's just that, you seemed so nice that day we interviewed you - I mean you still do - but I thought, we thought if we could just explain to her about the threatening letter, she might not be so upset.'

He smiles.

'I remember the interview.... it went better than the real one. Now let me get this right - you're involved in betting, skipping school, climbing trees to spy on people, poison pen letters - and you want me to speak to Kate Nantucket.'

I could crawl under the skirting board, I'm so embarrassed.

'... And you ran an excellent but unsuccessful campaign to stop them building on Turner's Meadow. I read that in the paper too. I'll see what I can do, how does that sound?'

He's off-beat alright, you can say that. It sounds brilliant.

We get to the door.

'You know, I don't really support your campaign,' he says, seeing us off. 'I can't see what the fuss is about. It's not exactly an area of outstanding natural beauty is it? In fact, it's an eye-sore if you ask me. But I'll do what I can.'

I weigh him up carefully.

'Remember when you had the tour round our place, with the other candidates...? What made you wear the socks?'

The sun's in his eyes.

'You noticed. Hmm. I suppose if the truth be known my heart wasn't really set on the job. Knew I could afford to quit you see, that was the trouble.'

'I thought it was something like that. You left us in the clutches of a little dictator instead. That means you owe us a favour.'

We leave him, standing in the sun.

PART 5:
KATE NANTUCKET

Chapter 21

Don't die of shock when I tell you this: Paul and I have been suspended. Absentee Appleby strikes again. Someone must have spotted us. I'm sitting at home with my letter, waiting for mum.

Mr. Dooley's resigned, too, poor devil. We heard this morning before I was sent for. I've never been so petrified in my life.

We're going down like flies.

I've introduced you to my dad haven't I, and his vile temper? Just warning you.

When the door goes my heart wangs against the bars of its cage. Mum bustles in rummaging.

'I've got a letter for you, from Mrs. Olney. What's all this about paying them a visit?'

'I've got one for you mum. Mr. Appleby. I think it might explain.'

We swap. I wish we could swap back and keep each other's.

'Oo, what's this - have you won a prize?'

No mum, not quite, just open it, please.

The shriek is audible several doors away.

*   *   *   *   *   *

I'm sitting on my bed gazing vacantly at my leg. There's a large red slap-welt on it, you can distinguish the fingers. Dad. First time since I was nine or ten, I can't remember, that he's actually hit me. He's gone out now, I keep expecting mum to come up and try and make amends, but she's probably had her instructions.

There's a knock later on, and quite a long pause before the stairs. Mum shows her in, stony-faced.

'Five minutes and no more.'

Adrienne.

'Sorry....'

First time I've seen her at a loss.

'You shouldn't have told about the Forge.'

'I know. I wish I hadn't. I was just so angry, the rat. Quite liked him, too, that's the annoying thing... Do they hit you? God. I don't get that. Sometimes I wish I did. I just seem to follow endlessly along behind the messes he makes.'

I look back at the leg.

'It's not your fault. Don't worry about it.'

'You were trying to get the concert back together, weren't you? I just came to say, if I can help....'

The letter. I'm still sitting on it. I rip it open.

'Sorry, forgot to get your name, but hope this will reach you via your mum. Kate will see you, but only briefly.

Two-fifteen Wednesday. Can you get permission from your head? Don't expect her to change her mind by the way. Good luck all the same. John Olney.'

God. That makes things a bit more interesting. Can you get permission. Ha.

'Permission from your head, that's rich. Do you want me to come? It might help, head's daughter and all that, you never know. She doesn't need to know he's totally bloody opposed to the whole thing, does she?'

I smile in spite of myself.

'What about school? I suppose he can't really suspend you, though....'

'That's not fair, I only offered. It was my idea in the first place, remember.'

She's right, I do. And it's more of a risk for her, not less.

'O.K. Wednesday, at the house.'

*   *   *   *   *   *

It's Mr. Threadgold who comes to the door. He's old, but his voice is strong and sure, like the house. We go past walls of books, a piano, grandfather clock, this is a serious dwelling. The lounge is lighter, the tree dominates the garden, yes, you would notice. There are paintings, and framed gold and platinum discs.

'Hi. Take a seat and tell me about yourselves.'

Beautiful. Commanding. Kate Nantucket.

Canadian accent.

Chapter 22

Seems like a lifetime since last summer but here we are again - all in the hall, the great shrouds of curtains are drawn back, the windows are open, dust dancing in the sunlight, young birds squawking, mowers, pollen. We made it. They've got the p.a. system up so we don't have to shut off the outdoors. This is the 'in-house' prize-giving, courtesy pupil-power. The great blue drugget's out so the first-years don't get their bottoms dirty sitting on the floor - mind, the drugget's not exactly sterile, you can hear the grit cracking as they go to their places. The rest of us are kind of tiered back, second and thirds on benches, fourth and fifth, chairs. Sixth standing, make that lounging, at the back. It's supposed to be informal, but obviously someone's coming, why else the delay?

They come in at last, from the back and down the aisle to a gasp and multiple swivelling of heads: Mr. Threadgold and guess who? Kate Nantucket's biographer, Mr. John Olney. He may not have got the job but he's made it to the stage anyway. Also one of the governors, I'm sure I've seen him before, sleek-looking chap with glasses. And Kate Nantucket herself - how sad in a way, she finally came. They mount the platform on a great rising cheer, and sit themselves by the table of house shields and the like.

There are no speeches, thank god, they just take it in turns to call the names and shake hands, the books won't get doled out till the proper evening do. They go through the years to ours. Claudia gets the French, surprise, and wins her seven p. English: my heartbeat quickens, to win and shake Kate Nantucket by the hand on stage with everyone there. Paul turns, row in front, I want to tell him I'll take Access but my mouth won't open.

The English prize, fourth year, to Adrienne Appleby.

She glides down the middle to wolf-whistles, and shares a joke on the platform. My eyes smart with disappointment, not to mention my pockets. I really thought I'd done it that time, she was so new and disorientated I didn't give her a chance.

Sucks.

They go on to the fifth and sixth, but I don't really hear. Oh *bum,* I didn't realise how much I'd set my sights on it, I just wanted to come out level with Liz once before I left that's all, so they could see it was me, not just her sister. She's got all the aces.

The governor steps forward to speak. There's a stunned silence. He's so different from the paper: it's not a governor at all - well, it is actually, he's been nominated now - it's our long-standing adversary, Mr. D. Humbolt.

For a sickening, giddy minute I think he's going to announce the plans to build have been cancelled, but they haven't. They've had a survey done and found our precious blades of grass are not vital to the ecological balance. To think, we spent all winter tiptoeing round them in the wet. But Humbolt's are making over a trust fund to finance our community projects for the next twenty years, no strings attached.

God, I'll be middle-aged then, maybe one of my kids'll be as brainy as Liz and go up for a prize.

The applause dies down and Mr. Threadgold steps forward to present Brendan with this year's community award. It's a beautiful silver globe on a plinth, bit like the Jules Rimet trophy without the player, if you're into football, we had it in the lounge the year Liz was head girl, I loved shining it, it was one of my jobs.

He says two names, Brendan and Kay - I'm going to be sick - Kay Downes. I'll never make it, I'll throw up.

On the stage, shaking his lovely great scrawny bear's-paw of a hand. He tells me, I think - the words break against my shore and get sucked back again - I have been honoured for my non-conformism. I am part of a tradition. We face the school and hold it together.

I made it, even if it was only for being a square, I think.

Wow. Me and Brendan. The whole school. We'll have to share - I'm sure we'll find a way. Shame about Janey.

If I can just make the steps without tripping.

Chapter 23

It turns out that Adrienne was more than just a county athlete with looks like a model, the pig, she also won the Smith's National Young Writers' Award one year - went up to London to get her cheque. Her winning entry was published in the anthology, it's in our library - if Janey had have done her job properly instead of accessioning and shelving Brendan she might have tipped me the wink and saved me a couple of pounds.

It didn't stop me telling Bowering I should have won the prize, though, it was alright that project, I don't care if I am biased. He said they had considered giving it to me but what spoiled it was it didn't seem to have a proper ending. Of course it didn't have a proper ending, I'm still writing it. They say you should write about the things you know best, well, this *is* what I know best. You're reading the last bit now.

I hope you've enjoyed it.

*   *   *   *   *   *

We had one final impeccable scene where we administered last rites to the Forge. It was the end of term, the day of the main prize-giving, the proper one. They had the doors wide open ready to gut it and go to work over the holidays. It didn't take long for a crowd of us to get down there, mostly fourth years the way it should have been, since we were the ones who made it all happen in the first place.

We were generally lounging in the sun, taking possession one last time. I was talking to Adrienne, having got over my envy, mainly on account of the community award, which was mounted in place of honour - Paul's place - the desk by the easel. They had me bring it in so we could be re-presented with it and take it back home, clever. She worked hard on her dad, Adrienne did, and eventually he saw the error of his ways, and made the move to contact Humbolt, first sensible thing he'd ever done I reckon, except getting this job here, that was sensible, we're not so bad all things considered. Apparently they got on from the word go, same taste in suits, probably.

But I hadn't finished telling you. We're sitting around savouring the last moments - Lindy's actually remembered her camera, looks quite odd taking snap-shots with her head-phones on - when we have a visitor. Mr. Olney. Fido.

'Thought I might find you in here,' he says. 'Someone to see you before they go.'

It's Mr. Threadgold, and Kate Nantucket. They stand in the doorway receiving our greeting and it's like they've come to somewhere they belong.

You can't get less formal than a disused glorified shelter where they dump broken desks, but it's still obvious the easel is the front, and the focus is where the trophy is, the silver globe, alight in the sun.

They make their way to it. There's just one word chalked up: FAREWELL. Mr. Threadgold's eyes are alive with sadness and understanding.

'My wife would have been proud,' he says, in his loving dog-voice. 'She always had faith in the young.'

There's a tissue-thin silence. No-one dares end it, or go. From inside me a voice says, quietly, to Kate

Nantucket, 'Would you sing that song, at the service, just once more?'

I'm mortified, in case I've spoiled it all.

She sits; with her hand resting on the globe she sings the song for us, in a way so intimate that it will live in our minds for ever. She has brought it home.

*   *   *   *   *   *

And so, although nothing really ends, it ends.

Brendan's gone, finally. Leeds Uni, of all places, doing Environmental Science - didn't quite get the grades he needed but scraped in anyway. I expect the community prize helped, ha, even if it didn't do too much for Turner's Meadow which now rests under a couple of hundred square yards of Humbolt's D.I.Y. store.

Ah well. It all went out in a blaze of glory, I suppose you'd have to say that. The concert was held on it, Midsummer's Night, they had a roped-off area where the helicopter landed and took off all night with the artists, courtesy of D.A. Humbolt Esq. who naturally had to descend from the summer skies in his biscuit-coloured Sainsbury's under-manager suit with Kate Nantucket herself, and make a little speech.

But it was brilliant really, watching it come in and out over the bands, ducking under the laser show like a dragon-fly, drowning the music.

There was even an album - Kate Nantucket: 'Meadowland'. It's her best, better than anything else, mellow and peaceful. It's not actually taken from the concert - they're all new tracks - but just the name's enough.

It was also the night Adrienne and Vlad got it together - who'd have thought in a million years? But I've got to know her quite well now, and I've noticed she's attracted to the risk-takers. And as risk-takers go, they don't come much bigger than Vlad. So it doesn't surprise me they're still an item.

But for me nothing will ever match the last gathering in the Forge. That was just for us.

As a matter of fact, Lindy took a brilliant picture of it, I've got a copy, from the back - it kind of leads your eye right through the watchers to Mr. Threadgold, and Kate, singing. You can recognise people even though their backs are turned. If you look you can see me nuzzled quite closely up to Paul, left-hand corner, on the same desk.

That's right folks, he finally got round to it, and it's all there on Kodachrome. Said he'd fancied me since the second year - think of all that time we missed. So it looks like Adrienne's not the only one to end up with a risk-taker. Well, I don't know about end-up, all I'm saying is, we're an item for the present and that's as far as it goes. We may be in the future, who knows? I'm not putting money on it.

That reminds me, a funny thing happened on my birthday. Card from Brendan. Written on both sides, mostly about the concert, various drinking feats at college and gossip about lecturers, but also hinting quite nicely that we might do worse than get together for a quiet drink when he was down for Christmas.

How ironic. All those years and years I dreamed and hankered for him, and I'm not even going to go. Besides, he's meant to be still on with Janey, is that what you call hedging your bets? I've no idea, and I don't think I'll be going along to find out.

*   *   *   *   *   *

It's my all-time favourite photo, everything that's ever mattered to me is in that shot. I had it blown up and spent most of that October's design lessons making it into a really professional poster. It's just this lovely grainy blown-up photo - the Forge, the song, and me and Paul, bottom left. And under it, in proper lettering,

KATE NANTUCKET PLAYS THE FORGE

Like I say, you have to choose your partners carefully with Kate Nantucket.

The End.

IN-SCHOOL DAYS

with Peter Hayden

PRIMARY

Primary School visits involve talks, readings, workshops, follow-up service (written comment on work done as a result of the visit), and signing session. There is a single fee, no extras, which includes presentation of books to the schools library.

The fee varies slightly according to travel distance, but is comparable to engaging cover for the day.

All books at signing sessions are well below cover-price.

SECONDARY

The visits involve talks and readings from 'The Great Premium Bond Swizzle' and other writing, including published work by teenagers. Writing workshops are geared towards exam and coursework needs if desired. The one-off fee includes signing session, follow-up service (see primary notes) and presentation of books to the school library.

The fee varies slightly according to travel distance, but is comparable to engaging cover for the day.

All books at signing are well below cover-price

INSET

Talks, demonstrations and workshops from the perspective of the child, teacher, and examiner, with extensive examples of children's work

For bookings contact Peter Hayden on 01299 824858, or contact Crazy Horse direct.

Publications available from Crazy Horse Press – no p&p, delivery by return, order form on back page.

The Adventures of Stringy Simon – Sampler

'His stories are very interesting, and one day he will get his books published and lots of people will buy them.'

'I liked the story when the two families went to America and met the President, and Rocky Racoon was sent to Stewart.'

'I liked the one about Accrington Stanley winning the Cup, it was really brill.'

'Not as good as Roald Dahl.'   *(Pupils, 8-12, various schools)*

Primary, £4.50 ISBN 1 871870 07 0

The Day Trip

'Gripped by the pace and realism of the writing we join the school outing and are bussed, sailed and decanted onto French soil. From now on, in spite of their luckless teachers, the kids are on their own, our lot rather more than the rest. Lost and late, they board the wrong boat home, merge with another school, and end up on the wrong side of the Watford Gap. Ah - but Mike and Lee have declared their love; and what a day they've all had. Hayden's an invigorating new talent to watch.'   *(The Guardian)*
Teens, £3.50 ISBN 0 19 271510 0

The Great Premium Bond Swizzle

'Lively, readable, eccentric - all the things I like ... I recommend it to anyone looking for a good footy read.'   *Nick Hornby*

'In racing parlance it could be said to have been bred by Nick Hornby out of Sue Townsend... it will appeal to all ages from adolescence onwards.'

'Flashing Blade' (Sheffield Utd. fanzine)

'A wonderful, charming and witty dose of escapist fiction... Highly recommended, even for us dour northerners.'

'Hey Big Spender' (Derby County F.C. fanzine)

'A football supporter's dream of a book... a heady mixture of wit and serious matter, the stuff of teenage lifestyle. Great stuff.'

'Fly Me To The Moon' (Middlesbrough F.C. fanzine)

'I greatly enjoyed *"The Great Premium Bond Swizzle"*, which made me laugh, and think, and deserves to succeed.'

Jill Paton Walsh

Adults & teens, £6.99   ISBN 1 871870 05 4

Against The Odds   ISBN 1 871870 02 X

George's Mechanical Sledge   ISBN 1 871870 03 8

I'm Seeing Stars   ISBN 1 871870 01 1

Man's Best Enemy   ISBN 1 871870 00 3

Four humorous stories written and illustrated by teenagers. 9-12 yrs., £5.99 - set of four.

Coming soon:

The Willy Enlarging Elixir & other stories

The second collection of Stringy Simon stories. Warning: contains rude material.

Upper primary & teen, £4.99   ISBN 1 871870 10 0

The Poppy Factory Takeover

Two humorous verse stories written by teenagers and illustrated by Clinton Banbury.

Teens, £2.99   ISBN 1 871870 08 9

Photocopy me!

Order Form: Complete and send to: **Crazy Horse Press,
116 Bewdley Road, Stourport, Worcs DY13 8XH.**
Please send me the following books by return:

.... copies of 'The Adventures of Stringy Simon'
@ £4.50 ....= £.........
.... copies of 'The Willy Enlarging Elixir'
@ £4.99 ....= £.........
.... copies of 'The Headmaster's Daughter'
@ £5.99 ....= £.........
.... copies of 'The Day Trip'
@ £3.50 ....= £.........
.... copies of 'The Great Premium Bond Swizzle'
@ £6.99 ....= £.........
.... copies of 'The Poppy Factory Takeover'
@ £2.99 ....= £.........
.... sets of 'Against The Odds', &c.
@ £5.99 ....= £.........

.....................TOTAL [no p&p required] . .= £.........

NAME ....

ADDRESS ....

....

.... POSTCODE ....

PHONE ....

I enclose a cheque for £ ....

Signed ....